METAL DEMON

Julie Hiner

Killers and Demons

First Printing in 2023

Publisher: Julie Hiner

KillersAndDemons.com

Editing by: Taija Morgan

Cover Design: Creative Paramita

ISBN: 978-1-7389176-1-7

First Edition

From deep within, this death metal meets demon possession was meant to be.

I dedicate this dark creation to Roland (Robbie) Doe, and to the origins of death metal: *Possessed, Death, Necrophagia, Obituary, Autopsy, Morbid Angel, Carnage, God Macabre, Entombed, Dismember, Grave,* and *Unleashed.*

CONTENTS

1. Cesspool — 1

2. Fireball — 5

3. Night Cap — 9

4. Hot Treat — 13

5. Depleted Metal Star — 17

6. Hunger and Thirst — 21

7. Forced Performance — 25

8. Starving — 31

9. Cinnamon Fire — 35

10. Sighting — 39

11. Lust — 43

12. Metal Struggle — 47

13. The Freshest Meat — 51

14. Demon Vision 57

15. Dine In 59

16. Demon Blood 63

17. On the Edge 65

18. The Needle 71

19. Mordis 77

20. Investigation 83

21. Morning After 89

22. Triple Header 93

23. Metal Saviour 97

24. Electric Passion 101

25. Aftermath 105

26. Accused 109

27. Grave Digger 111

28. Addict 115

29. Flesh Eater 119

30. Intervention 125

31. Call the Devil 135

32. Demon Ritual 139

33. Metal Demon Rise 143

34. Metal Men Unite 147

35. Dripping Eyes and Exorcist Tools 153

36. Killer Show	157

37. Heavy Metal Exorcism	165

38. Fresh Meal	171

Fullpage Image	173

Acknowledgments	175

About Author	177

Also By	179

Thank You	181

Cesspool

The death metal singer stood, boots rooted into the stage, long, wild hair sticking to his sweat-drenched face as he screamed into the silver bulb of the microphone. His deep voice seethed through the room, hypnotizing the manic crowd into a savage state, weaving tantric fingers through Elena's body. She'd consumed many metal singers, but she'd never felt tingles of lust before a meal. Something was *off*.

Heads banged the moist air, long hair flew, leather-and-chain-clad metal diehards clawed their way up onto the stage only to fling themselves into the open abyss, landing in a sea of alcohol-soaked hands. It was her first time dining on Soiled Carcass, and so far she was more than impressed by their high-voltage, raw-edged sound.

Elena breathed in the smell of the place. A serendipitous mix of blood, urine, and cheap booze. Her nostrils flared as she exhaled. Bad Idol was the perfect basement cesspool. Hiding in the shadows at the back of the dive joint, next to the bar, she scanned the crowd, stretching her tentacles over the situation. She liked to know the energy of a place before she submersed herself into her feeding.

This place felt good. The energy was wild. It was...*hair-raising*. She could really go for a good dose of high-frequency waves right about now. Her tank was dangerously low, the needle threatening to dip into the empty zone.

She sidled up to the bar and winked at the boyish bartender. He blushed, then snapped to attention. "What's your poison?" he asked.

Was he trying to be coy? Flirtatious, maybe. He'd be such a tasty little treat. A mere morsel. She could eat him up with a single snap of her jaws. First, she had to top up her fuel level. Recharge her battery.

"Fireball. Straight up." She smiled, licking her top cherry-red lip.

He set a shot glass onto the counter with a click, then filled it. Cinnamon and heat rose, weaving over Elena's face. She snapped a more-than-ample bill on the counter, then raised the glass in a toast. A toast to herself. To the state this place was in. To the state she would soon find herself in. She shot back the liquor and relished in the heat and afterburn.

Leaning against the sticky counter, she stared straight ahead. The savage crowd blurred into a fuzzy outline. None of them mattered. She was here for the front man, the demonic leader spouting his death metal lyrics. She scanned him slowly, taking in the details. His long, sandy-blond hair fell in thick waves. The hot stage lights cast psychedelic purples and blues over his bulging biceps. Sweat trickled down his muscular chest, dripping from his hardened nipples. His solid stance rooted him into the stage, his legs parted, his manhood protruding, stretching the tight pleather holding his flanks captive. Glimmers of gold etched the pleather down his legs, forming symbols of skulls morphed with overturned crosses. The heavy metal rings cluttering his fingers dug into the silver microphone shaft as he grasped it and poured out massive energy into each rough syllable. Raw lyrics spewed from his mouth, weaving through the air waves, reaching into the depths of her eardrums.

The metal god. He was the energy source in this basement pit. He was the one Elena was here for. He was the one she would feed upon.

FIREBALL

The burn of the third shot of Fireball tingled down Elena's throat. The aura in the basement-pit-turned-concert-hall heightened. Every air molecule infused her with a jolt of energy as it touched her skin. It was time. She couldn't go much longer without a meal.

She slithered away from the bar, her tall black boots catching glimmers off the pot lights, the chains hanging from her leather pants swaying against her curvaceous hips. She ran her gloved hands through the short spikes of her raven hair, preparing for her feast.

She made her way through the crowd cluttering together, closing in on the stage. Pushing aside scrawny beings coated in sweat and reeking of cheap liquor, drugs seething from their pores, she slipped through the ruffage toward the main dish.

She halted at the lip of the stage, dead centre. She raised her face toward the metal god. His rough vocals screeched into the pits of her ears. His wild gaze searched the crowd, landing on her. She closed her eyes and raised her arms.

The world inside the cesspool froze. The metal maniacs comprising the crowd halted mid head bang, mid hair whip, mid leap into the sea of waiting hands. The purple-and-blue pot lights heating the stage flickered. The rest of the basement pit went dark. Elena's body rose from the ground. Her eyes morphed into black holes. Streams of black ichor bled from her devil eyes, streaking her pallid cheeks. Hovering in front of the metal man, frozen mid screech, destined to be her meal, she took a deep breath in.

The cherry-red lips of Elena's mouth opened wide, parting into a sinister cavern. Her entire being inhaled. Every ion of her human form shimmered a hellish red.

A purple-blue essence seeped from the mouth of the metal god, through the sweat-infused air. In a glittering stream, it shot straight into the black hole that now stretched over half of Elena's face. The aura left the lead man, oozing from him in a fantastic stream of vibrant energy. Elena sucked it in, letting it replenish every particle of her being.

Black sludge bled down the walls. The room breathed. An icy chill trickled through the hot air, puffs of white streaking the darkness.

A blood-orange hue tainted the purple-blue stream feeding Elena's evil core. She shuddered. She closed her cherry lips and swallowed. The life essence streaming from the metal man dissolved.

A flash of light illuminated the entire room. Elena's toes touched the ground.

The crowd shuffled, the metal maniacs uneasy on their feet. Thoughts of *one to many* explaining away the collective moment of unsteadiness. The guitarist swung his arm, shooting out a guttural riff. Hands raised, heads banged the chill air, long hair flew wildly again. The metal god wavered; his voice shook. He found his balance, looking around him, stunned. He rejoined the height of the guitar riff with a screeching vocal.

Elena licked her lips like a well-fed lioness. His aura was like a high-end cut of beef, seared to rare perfection. She stared at the source of her meal. His emerald eyes darted over the crowd, landing on her. Their gazes locked. She narrowed her eyes and drank in his powerful stature. He'd been worth the effort. He might even be worth coming back for.

Some equated death metal with rotting energy. Satan. The *Devil*.

They had it all wrong. They were ignorant to where real evil resides. Demons are the ones that possess the aura of Satan. They are the ones that are filled with rotten, festering energy. Until they feast on the wild, savage, and pure energy that could only reside within a metal god perched upon his stage.

Night Cap

Elena spun on her heel and walked back to the bar. Time for a little treat to top off her evening. A night cap. A dessert. A cherry on the perfect sundae she'd sucked back like a platter of oysters. The hot sauce on the simmered meat digesting in the pit of her belly.

She leaned over the bar, hovering, waiting for the boyish bartender. He saw her from the corner of his eye and rushed over. "Another Fireball?"

"Nah. How about a nice after-dinner drink." She smiled.

"French Martini?"

"You have the mixings for that, in *this* place?" She twisted her lips into a smirk.

He chuckled. "No. But I make do. Johnny's version."

"Resourceful. Well, Johnny, how about you serve me up your version of a French Martini with your dive-joint ingredients." She sat on a stool, leaning her elbows on the bar, and ate him up with her eyes.

He smiled, showing a dimple, thrusting his boyish charm up several notches. "You got it."

He went to work on her cocktail. She watched him. His tight body, lean yet muscular, his chest rippling through his black t-shirt, his firm ass grinding against his jeans. What was he? Early twenties? Mid at best. She was technically too old for him, according to this physical body she was wearing, and the rules that this human society seemed to suffocate themselves within. She couldn't explain it. Ever since she'd pulled on this thirty-something skin tattooed with black dragons and pierced with silver studs, she'd been severely randy for young, muscular men. Boys, really. They were barely men by her standards, within the protocols of her world.

Her *beings.*

Tonight, the lust building in her human loins was beyond its usual simmer. It was the front man. It was as if he'd awoken something inside of her.

Johnny returned with a martini in hand, dimple exposed. "Here you go."

"Thank you, *Johnny.*" She put some sultry emphasis on his name. Dipping her cherry lips into the pink liquid, a maraschino bobbing against her mouth, she let the sugary liquor roll over her tongue. She swallowed. "Delicious."

"I'm glad you like it." Johnny smiled. "You didn't tell me your name."

Elena took another sip of liquor. "Elena." She licked her top lip. Why was she revealing her real name? She was all kinds of *off* tonight.

"Elena. Pretty name," Johnny said.

"You know how to compliment a woman."

He blushed.

"Say, what time do you get off, Johnny?"

"Show ends in fifteen. I'll probably be around another hour after that. These wild kids love a couple for the road."

"Well, suppose I stick around, walk you home."

He smiled, resting his elbows on the bar. "Sounds swell."

He was just too sweet for his own good. What was a girl to do? A girl with a ferocious appetite for metal god essence and boy-toy night caps.

Hot Treat

The sun shoved its bright rays through the thin white curtains hanging haphazardly over the streaked window. Heat seeped into the room, weaving hot tendrils over the covers, underneath the quilt, and into Elena's skin. She sat up and yanked them off.

Bloody Hell. Did it have to be so fucking hot in this top-level apartment?

She shuffled barefoot across the open space to the area designated as the kitchen. The studio apartment was one big room. She'd partitioned areas into living spaces. One for the bedroom. One for the kitchen. One for the TV room. One for her creative activities.

That was it. Four makeshift rooms and one tiny bathroom.

It was good enough for now. For as long as she'd be in this body. She'd become such an expert *invader* that she hadn't heard even the slightest *peep* from her hostess. Susan? No...Kate. No. *Pam.* Maybe. Some generic white-chick name, despite the interesting exterior of the human body. Elena had specifically chosen Pam, if that was her name, because Pam loved music and Pam dressed like a bad-ass rocker chick. Turned out Pam also had a convenient situation. She was a loner. Lived alone. Dined alone. Went to concerts alone. Except for her co-workers at Sam's Swap, the local record and cassette shop, she didn't interact with other humans. Elena had given Pam's notice at the shop on her behalf, claiming she was moving to another city. No one had knocked at the studio apartment door since Elena had moved in.

She grabbed a crumpled bag of coffee beans and poured some into a grinder. Sharp blades crunched beans, shooting a high-pitched whine through the room.

A groan erupted from the bedroom area. Elena jumped, snapping off the grinder. She looked over to the bed, witnessing shuffling under the covers, on the side of the bed she never slept on.

A boyish grin appeared, topped off with a dimple.

Double bloody hell. She'd forgotten about her late-night treat after her feast. *Jimmy? No. Johnny. Yeah. Johnny.*

She'd never let her night caps stay over. A sense of *offness* loomed. The chiselled face of the front man and his luscious locks shimmered across her thoughts.

"Good morning, Elena," Boy Toy chimed, slipping from under the covers.

What the metal fuck? Had she revealed her real name? A shiver cooled her hot demon blood as she thought about the last time she'd let her real name slip.

"Morning." Elena licked her lips. "Coffee?"

"That would be great." Johnny joined her in the kitchen, his abs rippling, his tight ass stretching his athletic boxers.

He looked just as delicious as he had last night, even without a Fireball and cheap-joint cocktail coating. Maybe she'd take another bite.

Blades sliced through beans as Elena pushed on the top of the grinder again. Spice wove through the small kitchen space. She poured the ground coffee into the machine and turned it on.

Johnny slipped his arms around her, from behind. She turned, his hot breath seeping over her face. Tingles burst through her borrowed body. She let it respond, leaning into Johnny. Images of their bodies entangled under the moonlight bathing the room through the large windows fluttered through her mind. He'd been good. She'd been extra charged, the lustful tremors she'd felt while drinking metal god aura lingering as Johnny brought her to several peaks. What could a little morning treat hurt? She'd have her way with him, then send him home before he suspected anything. He'd help her purge the forbidden thoughts from her feast.

Her lips met his, her body pushed against him, and she succumbed to the sexual hunger surging within the human form caging her soul.

Depleted Metal Star

S age rolled over in his bed and moaned. A steady pounding pulsed in the back of his head. Sliding long sandy-blond strands from his face, he looked up at the poster-collaged ceiling. The familiar visages of metal musicians stared down at him. What had happened? After the show he'd been exhausted. More than exhausted. Depleted in a way he could barely describe. Usually after a show he was exhilarated, riding the remnants of the high-voltage music and the wild crowd. Last night the crowd had been rough and raw. Savage, even. He'd relished in it.

A woman's face flashed through his mind.

He *had* relished in it, until he saw that woman weaving her way through the crowd, up to the stage. A bit older than the bulk of the crowd, she looked rough around the edges, like she knew how to give a man a real ride. Her cherry lips dripped experience. He figured she would exchange the appropriate services to join the band for their usual backstage party.

Sage paused, shuffling through the memories of the evening flashing through his mind. There was a gap. A period of time where his mind had gone blank. Wrenching his brain, he grasped for any remnant of the evening when he'd seen the woman. He remembered her face. Then blank space. The next thing he could recall, he'd been mid song, depletion weighing his body down like a dead weight pulling him to the depths of the ocean floor. Shark, his guitarist, had sidled over to him, nudging him with the toe of his signature red boots. As he came to and found his footing, he remembered Turbo shooting him a concerned glance from behind his shiny black-and-silver drum set, and Steele nodding at him, calloused fingers sliding down the thick strings of his black bass tipped in orange flames.

Sage had fought the heaviness, dug deep, and found enough energy to finish the show. As soon as they departed the stage and made their way to the back room where the party favours waited, he'd slumped onto the couch in the corner, too spent to even pour himself a shot. He hadn't felt that way since his heroine-infested decline toward triple rock bottom.

He slid his legs over the side of the bed. He wrenched his brain as he ran his hands through his long tangles. *Dammit.* Scanning the images of last night's afterparty flashing through his mind, he swore the woman hadn't followed him into his after-show life. He was sure he'd seen her, coming toward him, then in a flash she was gone. He'd been left clinging to the microphone, clawing at morsels of the energy flooding from his pores.

Why had he felt like the life had been sucked right out of him?

And what did the tattooed, cherry-lipped woman have to do with it?

He shook his head and shuffled across the room. He sounded crazy. How could a woman at the show who didn't even come to the afterparty have anything to do with his exhaustion? He walked into the living room and eyeballed the small pile of white dust on the coffee table, a razor blade and plastic bag nestled beside it. *What the fuck?* There was no way in metal hell he remembered doing anything other than burning shots of liquor last night.

He barely remembered stumbling into his apartment. When he'd said he was tired, Turbo had accused him of being a pussy. A washed-up old man. A wimp, unable to suck it up and party like the rock god he claimed to be. Steele and Shark had smirked and nodded in agreement. All three of them had loomed, waiting for him to respond. He'd shot back a double Jack Daniel's and forced his body to comply to his calling. He had a reputation to keep. And he'd be dammed if he'd be tagged as anything but the savage beast he portrayed on stage. But…this…this white powder. Someone must have come back to his apartment with him.

Four liquor-stained glasses cluttered the coffee table. Fuzzy outlines of his bandmates lingered in his mind. They *must* have come back here with him. That would explain the white death powder. He snatched up the glasses and walked to the kitchen. It must be the aggressive schedule they'd been keeping. They'd nearly tripled the number of shows they'd been doing in the last three months, and at least half had them hitting the road. Top that off with the liquor and groupie binge he'd been on, living the dream of death metal front man, and you definitely had a recipe for the perfect energy-depleting cocktail.

He grabbed a bag of dark roast from the cupboard beside the fire-engine-red fridge, humming strong and steady, and swore he'd take a several-day detox before the next show.

Hunger and Thirst

T rickles of light danced through the white curtains as they fluttered in the warm breeze flowing through the open window. Elena moaned as she rolled over, the warm spring air tickling her cheeks. She tried to swallow against the desert in her throat. Hunger clawed at her gut. Why was she so damn thirsty? And why was she hungry? It was far too early for that.

She opened one mascara-stained eyelid and looked at the neon-red numbers on the alarm clock perched on the chipped, antique nightstand.

She bolted upright. *Bloody hell.* How had she slept half the day away? She grabbed the clock radio and stared, both eyes wide open. The red numbers pulsed clear. 2:47 PM. She never slept this late. She had a schedule to keep. A feeding pattern that couldn't be toyed with.

Perhaps she'd been indulging too much. Not the feeding. She was sure she'd been keeping her metal-god-aura sucking to a strict pattern. No deviation.

But...the drinking? *Maybe.* The boy toys? *Probably.*

Or...was something else going on here? Since her last feeding on the lead singer of Soiled Carcass, she'd felt off. He'd triggered some strange sexual desire within her. She usually reserved that craving for her bartender boy toys. A demon had to draw some lines.

Shaking her head, she stood and grabbed a pair of bright-red sweatpants crumpled on top of a heap of clothes on the floor. Her fucking and feeding hadn't strayed from the lines. Even if they had, how could it possibly make a difference which humans she chose to feast on or to screw? They were all...humans. Homo Sapiens. The highest beings on the food chain. According to them. If only they knew. It was better they didn't. She couldn't imagine a world where her meals knew that they were...mere meals. Releasing a sigh, she continued to contemplate why it mattered. She'd been told the rules *imposed* upon her were for her own good. She was still a young demon, after all.

She slipped the sweatpants on, grabbed a white tank top off the same pile where she'd found them, and pulled it over her head. The material was soft and soothing on her skin. Her borrowed skin. Having real flesh was such a delight. She could feel *everything* in this skin. She loved it all. The tingles. The tickles. The prickles of pain.

She walked into the kitchen and grabbed the dark roast from the cupboard beside the baby-blue fridge. As she closed the cupboard, she glanced at the calendar stuck to the fridge with two matching Slave Grinder magnets. Slave Grinder. Now that had been a killer show. She'd never been so *quenched* from an aura. Scratches grabbed at her throat as she realized how thirsty she was.

A crash jolted her from her reverie as the coffee bag hit the sunflower linoleum and beans scattered across the floor. She froze, staring at the calendar. It had been a full week since she'd feasted upon Sage, the lead singer of Soiled Carcass, then took home Johnny and his dimple for a ride. Tonight. It was time to feast. Again. Tonight. She could have sworn she still had a couple of days. Yet, there was a red X striking out the entire week, leaving today the target for her feeding. Had she lost a couple of days? Had they vanished in a blur? She couldn't remember going to bed last night. She squinted at the square on the calendar marked Soiled Carcass. Something about the date pulled at her. Her eyes widened as it hit her. Her birthday. Her *demon* birthday. Six-hundred-and-sixty-six years. It felt like forever. Yet, she knew how young she was in the demon world.

Clenching her teeth, she picked up the bag and walked to the counter. Beans crunched under her bare feet. She didn't notice. Not even when a half-broken bean pierced the bottom of her foot. She left a trail of blood on the sunny linoleum as she shuffled in a stunned daze over to the grinder.

A growl erupted in the pit of her human body. *What the metal hell was going on?* She shouldn't be this hungry. She tried to swallow, but mere droplets of saliva slid down her parched throat. *Why so thirsty?* She yanked open a cupboard door, grabbed a glass, and thrust it under the cold-water tap. As she gulped it back, a twitching in her gut jolted her, causing her to spill down her tank top. *Damnit.* Something was moving inside of her. Could it be her hostess? *Fucking Pam.* This never happened. Could the hunger and the thirst be weakening her hold? She took a deep breath, closed her eyes, and summoned her demon energy. Another jolt of her human body as she slammed Pam back into her box. Her human body stilled. Her demon being settled.

She opened her eyes and exhaled.

She needed to get herself together. Fast. She couldn't even remember where she was supposed to go tonight. All she knew was that she had to feast. It would be an icy day in hell before she'd miss a feeding. The one time that had happened, she'd sworn she'd never let it happen again.

FORCED PERFORMANCE

S age sat at the bar at the back of the joint. Metal Panther was one of his favourite places to perform. Shark, Steele, and Turbo had pressured him to stay in the tiny back room behind the stage and crush Jack Daniel's until the show started. He'd made up some excuse about perusing the potential post-show treats that might be coaxed into joining the afterparty. The truth was the tiny dressing room was closing in on him. Suffocating. And his bandmates were irritating. Their incessant chatter seemed amplified. As Turbo left his usual even-tempered vibe and thrust into overdrive, his voice seemed even higher pitched than normal. His shoulder-length hair bounced around his broad shoulders as he jerked his body around like a jackass. And their odour. Hail to the metal gods, their odour was something unbelievable tonight. As Steele pulled his long, dark hair up into a knot, the sweat trickling down his pale face and pooling under his armpits made Sage cringe. Shark was the worst. His usual glossy blond waves looked oily and a stale smell seemed to seep from his pores.

He couldn't understand what was happening. Were they always this loud and this disgusting? Or were his senses in overdrive?

Whatever it was, he had to get out of that tiny room.

With another hour before the opening act, the place was only sparsely populated. He'd easily made his way to the bar without being recognized. He stared at the vodka and soda he'd been nursing for nearly half an hour and wondered what was wrong with him. He'd ordered his usual, Jack Daniel's, straight up. The taste had made him gag. The vodka seemed less offensive, and the soda was settling his stomach. What the fuck was going on? Couldn't be nerves. He never got anxious before a show. Exhilarated, maybe. Nervous, never.

He'd only been detoxing for the previous six days, since the last show. His system was cleaned out. But it wasn't enough to cause all his senses to reach hypersensitivity. Was it?

Lately, they'd been doing double shows every weekend, and often sliding one in mid week. He'd been so depleted after their last one, he was relieved they had a short break. Normally, he wanted to play as much as possible. Keep the wheels greased. Keep his vocal cords on a constant hum. It had taken a lot to get Soiled Carcass into full swing. With two albums released in the last year and steady shows on the local music scene, he refused to let them lose momentum. He knew he might be pushing too hard, but he wanted to keep their fire lit. He'd been worried about burning them out. Seems like he was the only one feeling it.

He still couldn't get that woman out of his head. The woman with cherry lips and dragon tattoos weaving through the crowd at the last show. He couldn't get it out of his mind that she was linked to the severe depleted state he'd found himself in smack in the middle of the show. Every time he relived the feeling of clawing his way back into the song, the show, her face flashed into his mind.

He'd spun wheels thinking and rethinking it over. He came to the same conclusion every time. It was impossible she'd had anything to do with it. She hadn't been at the afterparty. He'd had no physical contact with her whatsoever. The only explanation, logical explanation, was that with all his pushing to keep Soiled Carcass climbing the ranks of metal's stars, he'd run himself down. Mix in the sex, double-show, and booze bath he'd plunged himself into, a man can only take so much.

It had been almost a full alcohol-free week. He'd drowned his insides with lemon water and fresh salads. He slept well every night. Hell, he'd even gotten fresh air every day. He had no idea there were so many forest trails in his city.

His clean state must be the reason the loud chatter and stench of his bandmates had gotten to him. And why his usual friend, Jack Daniel's, had turned bitter on him. It made sense.

Yet, something nagged at him. He had detoxed before. He was always a little more sensitive after. For a couple of days, anyways. But not like this. The mere taste of his pal JD had never let him down. The smoky oak. The afterburn. The longtime relationship had been the only one he could count on.

He stared at the glass of vodka and soda, frowning in disapproval of the fresh bubbles bursting to the surface of the clear liquid. What was wrong with him?

Fuck it.

He waved over the bartender. Her candy aroma engulfed him from several feet away.

"Another?" Her pink lips twisted into a playful smile.

His insides relaxed. "Jack Daniel's please. Straight up." He smiled back.

"You got it, sweet stuff."

As she walked away to tend to his order, his insides relaxed. He was overthinking all of it. He simply needed to rekindle his relationship with JD and flirt a little with this hot bartender. Yeah. A couple drinks. A little love from the server. Then get backstage and get pumped up with his bandmates.

"Here you go, sweet stuff." The bartender leaned over the bar, her milky breasts spilling from her sheer top.

"Thanks." He took a long sip, closing his eyes, letting the flavour take over all his senses.

He opened his eyes. She was still there, watching him.

"My pleasure." She smiled, a dimple appearing below her right cheek. "I know who you are." Her cheeks flushed as she giggled. "You're the lead singer of Soiled Carcass."

"You got me." Sage took another sip of his drink. His energy slowed to a zen flow.

"Damn. Can't wait to see you on stage tonight."

"Busy after the show?"

"Depends. Who's asking?" She giggled.

"I am." He leaned over the bar, his face inches from her, her aroma intoxicating him.

"Well, in that case, my schedule's wide open." She winked.

He pulled a laminated card from his back pocket and slid it across the bar. "For you."

She picked up the card, her eyes widened. "Backstage pass to your private party. I'll be there, sugar."

"I'm counting on it." He shot back the rest of his drink.

"Another?"

"Why not? One more for good luck."

She turned away. He sat there watching her, his insides relaxing more with each breath of her perfume. His entire being had settled down several notches. He was in a good place. The best place he'd been in since the day of his last gig. Turbo was amped up for the show, and his energy drove Steele and Shark up a notch. Shark had even polished his red boots till they shone. Steele had opted for a fresh pair of leather pants, sooner than usual. Sage decided he needed to ride the same train. All he had to do now was get pumped up. Pull off a killer set. Then relish in post-concert treats.

Starving

The place stunk of mold.

Elena hovered by the door, scanning the crowd. Usually, these places smelled like cheap beer. Potent liquor. Smoke and sweat. The worst ones were clouded in hot body odour with a metallic tinge.

This place smelled like wet and rot.

Was something off? Or was she overreacting?

She didn't have time to case out another joint, so she walked up to the bar. A drink, or two, would take off the edge. She'd settle in, drink in her meal, then go home. Tomorrow would be a new day. Fed, full and rested, things would look bright and promising once again.

A young bartender, blonde curls, pink lips, slid up behind the bar as Elena took a seat.

"What can I get ya, sweet stuff?"

A cloud of candy aroma drifted across the bar. Elena smiled. "Fireball. Double." Her usual routine was off. She usually arrived early, had a few drinks, took in the essence of her meal from afar before her feast. And now this young, female treat hovered in front of her. Not her usual choice for dessert, but along with the growing hunger throbbing in the pit of her belly, her sexual desire was swelling in sync with the thirst parching her throat.

"Here ya go, sweet stuff." The blonde bartender set the double Fireball on the counter and winked.

Elena's insides rumbled. She shot back half the cinnamon fire in a single gulp. She turned to face the stage. Carnal Assault should be on any minute. Or was it Rancid Cross? Elena shook her head and shot back the other half of the tumbler in a single gulp. The cinnamon-spicy-fire tickled her throat and titillated her senses. Hunger pains clawed at her belly like angry unkempt fingernails. She wasn't sure what time it was or whether the opening band had already played.

Tonight, she'd struggled to get her senses straight. She still couldn't believe she'd slept half the day away. Even after several cups of coffee and a couple litres of water, her thirst hung in her throat like dry sand. It was such a *human* sensation, totally foreign to her. To top that off, her hunger had built to a steady grumble in the pit of her belly. She usually got peckish a couple hours before her feeding. She hadn't felt hunger this strong in a long time.

She stared at her empty glass.

She'd hang here. Have a couple more drinks. She'd have to settle for the next act, headliner or not. As soon as they took the stage, she'd take in the essence of her meal from afar for a couple of tracks, three at most, then unleash her hunger. She knew she'd feel better once tonight was behind her. Yeah. Hang in there. She could do it. Live with this growling pain in her gut for a little bit longer.

"Can I buy you a drink?" a soothing, deep voice interrupted her thoughts.

She twisted her neck toward the cloud of Drakkar Noir wafting from beside her. Her breath caught. A twenty-something boy, *man,* stood, near enough for her to breathe him in. He leaned an elbow on the bar, hovering close to her face. His eyes were dark. Like obsidian. His skin was like milk. His hair, slicked back, shone under the dim lighting. His chiseled sculpture of a body toyed with her senses. Every cell in her body screamed for the pleasure she knew he could bring to it. She swallowed against the desert scratching the back of her throat.

"Sure." She bit her bottom lip, trying to restrain herself from ravaging him right here.

Her randiness, thirst, and hunger had all amplified in unison. Growing exponentially with every second. Taking over her every thought.

Tonight, she *had* to satiate them all. Her hunger. Her thirst. Her sexual desire.

The answer to the latter stood right in front of her.

Cinnamon Fire

A roar from the crowd erupted through the joint. Both Elena and her newfound treat, Jake, turned and stared at the stage. Purple smoke plumed up the stage, seeping across the room, wrapping them in a sugar mist. Jake slid a tumbler half full of red lusciousness toward her.

"Cheers." She lifted the glass as he lifted his, then shot back the cinnamon fire.

The crowd erupted as Carnal Assault launched into their fourth track. Their leader stood at the lip of the stage, his long charcoal hair shimmering under golden pot lights, his slate eyes searching the crowd. Elena had promised herself to take in their essence from afar for three tracks, then feed before her hunger got out of control. She couldn't pull away from the hold that Jake had on her. His dark eyes and Drakkar Noir scent intoxicated her. He was dangerous. She felt every bit of control slipping from her fingertips.

Pain gripped the pit of her belly. Despite having downed three double shots of Fireball, nails scratched down her throat with every swallow. The thirst thriving inside of her was too much.

A high-pitched wail vibrated through the crowd. A high-voltage riff echoed through the room. The crowd screamed. The temperature shot up. The riff came to a dramatic end.

The Carnal Assault lead singer immediately launched into the next track.

Elena's gut grumbled. Her throat scratched. She couldn't wait any longer.

She turned to Jake. "I love this song. I'll be right back."

"Sure thing." He winked at her.

She slithered her way through the packed crowd, pushing at slippery arms. She made her way toward the centre of the stage. There he was. The lead man. The one she was here to feast on. She stood for a moment, staring up at him. Charcoal strands flew wildly around his head, sticking to his slick face. Slate eyes explored the crowd, landing on her. It was now or never.

She raised her hands into the air. The room darkened. The crowd slowed. Elena's arms shook. Her hold on the room was weak. She could sense movement in the back corners. Willing her demon energy to heighten to full power, her human body trembled. The pain in her stomach clenched her human flesh. She couldn't wait any longer.

Her feet lifted, her body rose. Her human form, heavy against her dwindling demon energy, refused to rise any further. She opened her mouth, forming a pit with her cherry lips. She breathed in long and hard. The metal man responded. His mouth opened wide as he belted out the next lyric. He froze. A green-yellow shimmer burst from his lips, formed a glimmering stream, shooting across the room. The aura plunged straight into Elena, filling her up. She shivered. Her eyes fixed on his. Her lips open, her mouth receiving, sucking the life force, Elena drank, and drank, and drank. Thick black fluid dripped from the ceiling, crawling down the walls. Her mind jolted, telling her to stop. Her body craved more. She tried to swallow. She clenched her jaw in an attempt to shut her mouth. What was happening? She continued to drink, beyond the point of saturation. All control had vanished. Her own voice screamed through her mind. *Stop. Stop. Stop!*

Her jaw snapped shut. Her boots hit the ground with a loud thud. The voice screaming inside her head to stop went silent. The yellow-green shimmering aura pulled back, vanishing into the lead singer's mouth. Elena jolted. She shook her head, coming to her senses. She stared at the stage.

The lead singer's mouth snapped shut. He dropped to the ground. The microphone flew from his hand, landing on the floor with a thud. High-pitched feedback squealed through the room. The crowd gasped. The guitarist continued to pump out a raw riff as he shuffled over to the lead singer.

The crowd recovered, thinking it was part of the show, or part of the life of a metal god. The guitarist nudged the singer with his boot. The singer teetered on his heels, pulling his charcoal hair away from his face, looking up at the guitarist. He stood, wavered, then found his balance. The guitarist moved back to his side of the stage, amping up the voltage on the riff. The lead man found the microphone, stood tall, took a deep breath, then belted out the next lyric. The crowd went manic. The room vibrated with fresh, savage energy.

Elena jumped into action. She needed to get the fuck out of here. Now. She lowered her head and wove her way through the crowd. Complete satiation settled over the pit of her gut. No grumbling. No hunger. Her insides pulsed with satisfaction. She slowed her pace as she reached the back of the joint.

Drakkar Noir was still at the bar. He was watching the stage, nursing a drink.

Elena paused. She needed to bolt. She'd overdone it. Drunk too much of the singer's essence. She'd nearly maimed him. She had to get out of here.

Her thirst continued to swell in the back of her throat, along with the tingling desire in her loins. She needed complete satiation before the night ended.

Why not take her dark-eyed treat with her?

She detoured toward the bar.

SIGHTING

The relationship between Sage and Jack Daniel's was on the mend. After several drinks at the bar with a side of intense flirtation with the pink-lipped bartender, he'd felt like himself again. He'd watched Carnal Assault perform their first few tracks. They sounded good. Better than an opening act. The lead singer, up on stage, belted out raw lyrics. His voice was deep and soothing with an edge. This guy was good. Real good. Sage hung around until their third track ended, then slipped an ample stack of bills into the hand of the bar-tender, letting his fingers linger on her skin. She'd blown him a candy kiss as he stepped away from the bar. He walked along the edge of the joint, back against the wall, keeping his distance from the crowd, drinking in the voice of a fellow metal god.

Not far into the fourth track, the singer suddenly seized and crumpled to his knees. The crowd seemed to be in some sort of paralyzed trance. The room had darkened. A fluid dripped from the ceiling down the walls. A strange stream of cosmic colour swirled through the space.

In a flash, the singer came to. The crowd began to move. The rest of the band shot confused glances at the singer, then at each other. The guitarist led them into a rough-edged melodic detour, waiting for the singer to come out of his trance. The guitarist walked over to the singer and nudged him with a heavy boot. The singer's body shuddered as he came to, scanning the crowd, looking like he was lost. As he got his bearings, he grabbed for the microphone, stood tall, and belted out the next lyric.

The crowd went manic.

Sage scanned the sweaty patrons, trying to figure out what had happened. It was the strangest thing he'd ever seen. It wasn't the way a body reacted to too many shots or drugs. It reminded him of how he'd felt up on stage at their last show, when he lost time.

A dark-haired woman with tattoos caught his attention. She was making her way to the bar. A chill trickled down Sage's back. The woman stopped suddenly and turned to talk to a young man. The side of her face was visible. Sage gasped. It was the same woman he saw at their last show, right after he came to from his momentary blackout. At the exact moment he'd felt the extreme depletion. It was her. The same cherry lips. The same spiked black hair. The same dragon tattoos crawling over her pale skin. He was sure of it.

He should go talk to her. Find out who she was. And what the fuck she had to do with what happened to him the other night.

He shook himself from his reverie and walked along the outside of the crowd.

The tatted-up rocker chick started walking toward the back door, the dark-haired man following.

Sage picked up his pace. He needed to close in on her before she got to the door.

The woman turned her head, catching Sage's gaze.

Sage lunged forward.

The woman took the dark-haired man's hand and pulled him toward the back door.

A hand grabbed Sage's arm.

"Hey man, we need you backstage." Shark's blond waves looked glossed up again, his blue eyes narrowed with concern.

"Yeah." Sage shot his gaze back toward the door. He scanned the crowd. There was no sign of the woman.

"Turbo's out of control, man. You gotta come, *now,*" Shark pleaded. He turned and charged forward, his signature red boots clanking against the hard floor.

Sage nodded and followed Shark. Turbo was the most even-keeled of the band. That small percentage of the time when he got riled up, it took a split second for him to go into overdrive. His mind whirled with images and thoughts. The sweat pouring down Steele's face. The high pitch of Turbo's voice. The stale smell seeping from Shark that now seemed to have vanished. The woman with cherry lips and spiky black hair. The lead singer of Carnal Assault, crumpled on the stage. The blank spot in his own mind during the show the other night. This couldn't be a coincidence. This woman, at two different shows, at the very moment a lead singer crumples. What was the connection?

Lust

Elena arched her back as she grasped the edges of the white fur rug. Tequila slid between her breasts, mixing with her sweat, and his, into an animalistic cocktail with the scent of sex. Her Drakkar Noir-doused boy toy leaned over her and slid his tongue up her torso, between her breasts, lapping up the sweat and alcohol.

The young ones. They had stamina. This one also had skill. He knew exactly how much pressure to apply in the precise position. Tingles erupted between her thighs and migrated down her legs like electric shocks.

The Soiled Carcass singer from the other night, his luscious blond locks and rippled torso, kept flashing through her thoughts. She hadn't felt right since she'd fed on him. Usually, she could focus completely on her after-dinner treat, keeping her hunger and her lust separated. Since her feeding last week, her senses had heightened and blurred into a single throbbing desire to eat, drink, and fuck.

Her current dark-haired boy toy crawled over her, finding her and moving into her. She breathed in his essence. Fresh. Young. Vibrant. She wasn't supposed to feed on his type. Hunger clawed at her insides, despite the out-of-control feeding she'd indulged in less than an hour ago. What damage could a little taste do? Mid thrust, his manhood hard against her human pleasure spot, she opened her mouth, forming a dangerous cavern. His mouth responded. Blood-orange shimmers of light streamed from him, into her. She closed her eyes and breathed him in. Several hits later, he gasped. She opened her eyes. His pale face hovered over hers. His eyes wide, his flesh sickly. She'd gone too far. Taken too many hits of his essence. She was losing him. There was no turning back now.

She clamped her legs around his back, pulling him closer. His manhood probed further into her human point of bliss. Tantric tingles erupted through her insides and down her legs. Her cherry lips turned blood red as they spread open, exposing the cavern of hunger within. She inhaled.

The air between her mouth and his took on a rust-burgundy hue. His face whitened until shades of blue ate his skin. He went limp. His body pressed into hers.

Her body jolted with his vibrant essence. Energy sizzled through her veins. She pushed him off and sat up, stretching out her arms, her legs, allowing the fresh life to sizzle every pore.

She stood and looked down at his lifeless body.

Bloody hell. Hunger and lust had taken control. She crouched and pressed two fingers into his neck. Nothing. She'd killed him.

This was way beyond the rules.

What would she do with him? No one knew where he was. He'd ditched his friends. She'd convinced him to turn off his phone. There was no trace. She could dispose of him, quickly and quietly.

Maybe she could keep her fuck-up a secret.

Metal Struggle

The energy of the crowd was in overdrive. Their hungry eyes looked up at Sage as they devoured every word he sung and every morsel of energy he pumped into the performance. They were a vicious crowd tonight, thirsting for more, no matter how much he gave them.

As he launched into the opening words of the last track of the night, he wondered if their appetite was larger than usual, or if he was running on empty. He'd detoxed for several days after his complete depletion at the last show. He'd taken his foot off the gas and put a hold on the metal-booze-sex binge of non-stop shows they'd been hammering out. Still, he'd felt tired backstage before the opening act had started. He'd forced his relationship with Jack Daniel's, rekindling it before it was too far gone. The candy scented bartender had helped. When Shark had pulled him backstage to deal with Turbo, his energy had returned. He thought he was back to normal. His normal. The normal of a raging metal god. Now, he wondered if it had been the excitement resulting from the situation.

When he caught site of the tattooed, spiky-haired woman, his adrenaline shot up. He couldn't shake the instinctive feeling she had something to do with his depletion at his last show. It was too much of a coincidence that she was there tonight at the very moment the lead singer of Carnal Assault, Dagger, had crumpled to the stage. The look seeping from Dagger's eyes shot Sage back to the moment that he had lost all motion, all thought, all memory, as he belted out vocals on centre stage.

Backstage, he saw Dagger and asked him if he was all right. Dagger shook his head, claiming it was the weirdest thing ever. Sage took a risk and asked him about the woman. Confusion riddled Dagger's face as he had nodded and said he saw the woman in the crowd as he was coming to. Dagger asked Sage if he knew her. Sage told him he didn't, but he'd seen her too, in the crowd. Declaring it was fucking weird and he was ready for a shot, Dagger moved on, leaving Sage more confused than ever.

The cherry lips and pale face clung to his thoughts, even now as he fought to stay focused on his performance.

He sung the last word of the chorus. Shark stepped up to the centre of the stage, glossy blond waves shining under the iridescent lights, thrusting his metallic-blue guitar in the air and launching into a killer solo. Sage stepped back, toward the shiny drum set and gave Turbo a devil's horns with his mic-free hand. Turbo's brown hair bounced around his broad shoulders and sweat soaked his black tank top as his muscular arms thrust an assault on the drums.

After the pre-show intervention, Turbo had eased up and settled himself in time for their set. Sage grabbed a bottle of water from the lip of the stand elevating the drum set and took a long swig. After chugging half the bottle, he felt slightly replenished. Walking toward his prime spot, he looked over at Steele. Heavy hands sliding over the thick strings of his black bass tipped in orange flames, Steele nodded as his long, dark hair whipped wildly.

Sage scanned the crowd, inspecting each face, looking for her. As they pumped out a high-energy set, Sage realized they'd have to have a talk. Tomorrow. When everyone was lucid. They still had several more weeks to complete the aggressive tour they'd committed to. They were so close, the last thing Sage wanted was for them to have to cancel any show.

The guitar solo ended. Sage lifted the microphone, took his place at the very tip of the stage, dead centre, and streamed all his energy into belting out the last round of the chorus. As his voice morphed into a death metal screech, he released the last words of the song. The drumbeat went manic. The electric guitar riff followed. The crowd went savage. The last mosh pit enthusiasts of the night flung themselves through the air. Sweat, booze, and adrenaline doused the sticky air.

Sage pumped his fist, saying his thank you and his farewell to his beloved crowd. He walked backstage, Shark, Steele, and Turbo in tow.

Exhaustion, mental and physical, took over his mind and his body.

He needed to figure out what was wrong with him—and fast, before the next show.

The Freshest Meat

Elena stood over the white fur rug looking down at the rippling muscles and tight physique of the young, dark-haired man. His Drakkar Noir scent was quickly drowning in a metallic odour. Every ion in her body buzzed with electric energy. She'd *never* felt this good before, in this borrowed body. She'd also *never* sucked the life aura out of two humans in one night, she'd never ventured from her *meal type,* and she'd never gone far enough to *kill.*

She'd been playing it safe, following the rules. Of all the situations she'd been given, assigned to, chosen, this one was her favourite. The thirty-something, tatted-up, bad-ass, rock-chick thing was really working for her. It suited her sassy essence. Her feeding grounds, the live shows in seedy joints, had been *delicious.* She loved the feel of these places. The *smell* of them. They were so raw, so real.

She grabbed her clothes scattered over the floor and walked to the bedroom area. Dropping the leather and chains into a pile on the floor, she walked over to the armoire and slid her silk housecoat off a hanger. Slipping her arms into the soft material, she looked across the room at the lifeless body.

She was out of control.

At the show, she'd gone too far with the metal god. She distinctly remembered trying to stop sucking the life aura out of him, and her body refusing to comply. That had never happened to her before. Now, here, in her borrowed body and equally borrowed apartment, she'd killed a man. She was a life-essence-sucking demon, living under the radar in a human world. Murder could bring unwanted attention. The last time she'd gained too much attention, she'd nearly been exorcised. It would be a frosty-tipped day down below before she'd let that happen again.

A tiny claw of fear scraped the back of her throat.

Would *he* know?

She shook her head. *No.* This wasn't the time to go down a maze of wild thoughts and worry. She needed to get to work and remove any sign of this dead man bleeding out on her white fur rug.

She'd need to cut him up. He was far too big for her to easily dispose of. He'd need to be broken down and packaged.

She sifted through the kitchen cupboards, trying to find a knife strong enough to cut human flesh and cartilage. It wasn't something *her type* of demon usually needed. The agreement was that she would keep herself fed by drinking the aura of metal gods. It was quite specific. She would only drink enough to keep herself replenished. She would stick to a strict feeding schedule. No murder would occur.

An icy tremor ran through her veins at the thought of explaining this to *him*.

She shook the thought from her mind. There *had* to be something here she could use. After searching every cupboard, at least twice, Elena leaned against the counter and wracked her brain, trying to figure out what to do.

Out of desperation, she walked over to the softly humming fridge and flung open the cupboard over head. Thank the metal gods. A knife block with three knives protruding from it perched in the high cupboard. Standing on her tiptoes, she slid the largest knife free. Moonlight trickling from the window glinted off the blade as she turned it over. It would have to do.

Despite the double-aura dinner she'd had, and the two-time lustful satisfaction before putting her latest treat to his end, she was ravenous. And thirsty. *So thirsty.*

She set the knife on the counter. After gulping back two cups of water, she felt invigorated enough to proceed.

She'd never felt this insatiable.

Clutching the handle of the knife, thirst rising in her throat as she walked toward her dead boy toy, she halted. She was so hungry, so thirsty, her mind wasn't functioning properly. She couldn't very well leave a mess, now, could she? She had to do her best to hide all traces of it.

Sprinting back to the kitchen area, she set the knife aside, opened a drawer, and lifted out a roll of Saran Wrap. It would have to do. She figured several layers of it might work.

After pulling a dozen long sheets from the roll and plastering them, stacked on top of each other, to the floor, she walked back over to the man. He was on the rug, but not that far from the linoleum at the edge of the kitchen space. She crouched down and heaved him over onto his side. Rolling him slowly inside the fur rug, she got him onto the plastic wrap.

Perfect.

The only blood was on the white fur.

She stood, slid her housecoat off. The sweat dripping down her neck and her back cooled.

She stared at the man. Poor Jake.

Time to get to work.

She grabbed the knife. Gripping the handle tight in her right hand, she pressed her left hand against his shoulder, and began to saw, just below the shoulder bone. Something told her this was the way to cut a body, human or otherwise, into pieces. It was very much like carving a chicken. If you got the blade in that sweet spot where the bones connected, you could slice right through at the joint. It was much easier, and cleaner than cutting through bone.

As the blade sliced into his flesh as if it was butter, Elena's mouth watered. Fresh blood burst from the slice, oozing over his flesh. A droplet of saliva trickled from the corner of her mouth and dribbled down her chin. As the limb came free, dropping back onto the plastic, she inspected the fleshy internals. The bright red of the raw meat taunted her. She licked her lips. It took everything within her to hold back from gorging herself.

She shook her head and lowered the knife. What the hell was wrong with her? She was an aura-sucking demon. She *wasn't* a flesh eater. Bile crawled up the back of her throat at the thought.

A hint of fear attached itself to an image of human flesh creeping from a crevice of her mind.

She raised the knife again, willing herself to get on with it. Using all her will power, she focused on the precise cuts between the joints, and placed each piece of meat in a row along the plastic wrap sticking to the floor. She moved into some sort of strange flow, somehow knowing what to do. Once he was sliced cleanly into thirty-four pieces—two lower legs, two upper thighs, two feet, ten toes, two upper arms, two lower arms, two hands, ten fingers, a torso (the biggest piece), and a head, she stood and admired her meticulous work.

Again, she wondered how she had been able to cut him up so precisely.

The hunger within her swelled. The building thirst gripped her throat.

All she could think about was biting into the raw flesh and the moist blood soothing her throat.

As her lips grazed the chunk of meat wet against her palm, she jolted. The flesh hit the floor with a wet thud, sending sprays of red through the air. A droplet landed on her arm. Saliva swam through her mouth.

What the hell was happening? She'd broken enough rules already within a matter of hours. What would happen if she *ate flesh?* She was supposed to stick to drinking life essence. She was supposed to be *hands off.*

Her naked body, coated in a sweat gloss, pumped with adrenaline.

She walked to the sink, thoroughly rinsed the knife, and pulled out a bottle of lemon-scented Palmolive, giving the blade a good douse. After rinsing the knife and wiping it dry with a floral tea towel, she walked back over to the block and slid it securely within.

She scanned the cuts of meat, lined up on the plastic wrap. The supply would last her a while.

What was she thinking?

Was she *really* going to eat flesh? She was in *this* borrowed body playing the role of metal-god-aura-sucking demon. She *should* be afraid of the consequences.

Right now, all she could think about was the insane hunger and thirst rising within her.

Demon Vision

S age bolted upright in bed. Cold air wafted from above, ici-cle kisses dotting his cheeks. Sweat-drenched golden locks stuck to his shoulders as he tilted his head back and looked up. A face glowed. Pallid flesh stretched across a hundred-year-old face. Black ichor dripped from dark caverns where eyes should be. A black mouth twisted and contorted, the expression impossible to read.

This was real. It had to be.

A thick, black droplet stretched down on a thin thread toward his face. It broke free, landing on his skin with a splat.

He couldn't be dreaming, could he? He shook his head, blinked hard, then looked back up.

Nothing. It was gone.

His eyes roamed over the brown stains dotting the stucco ceiling. He shivered. Droplets of cold moisture drizzled down the back of his neck. What had he seen? Why was he so cold?

He wiped his cheek, then looked at his hand. A smear of black oozed over his fingers. It *was* real.

Yanking the sweat-drenched sheets aside, he slipped off the mattress and trudged across the room. The small space glowed with a haze from the moon reaching its silver fingers through the window.

Sage opened the curtains and rested his forehead against the pane. The cold glass soothed his hot skin.

Scanning the quiet streets, he wracked his brain for some kind of explanation as to what was happening to him.

Was he going insane?

He trudged to the kitchen, grabbed a tea towel, and wiped his hand and his cheek. Black smeared the flower-patterned cloth. If he was flying off the mental rails, then why did this all seem so real?

Dine In

The studio apartment filled with the smell of fresh, lean meat as a fillet sizzled in a cast-iron skillet. Elena leaned against the counter, flipper in one hand, glass of red in the other. She took a long, luxurious sip of the scarlet liquid. It was luscious. The best red she'd ever tasted. It should have an expensive price tag attached to it, however, the way she had acquired it had cost her nothing. At least, so far.

She turned to the pan and flipped the meat over. Perfectly browned with a caramelized coating, it was minutes away from perfection. She was in the mood for medium-rare. She didn't understand this craving for human flesh. For blood.

It had grown into a raging hankering for a perfect medium-rare fillet. Since she had an entire beast butchered, packaged, and shoved into the tiny freezer comprising the top third of the refrigerator, she could satisfy a craving for any cut of meat. At least for now, until her supply diminished.

She took a few more sips of the red, watching the meat, then turned the stove top off and transferred the fillet to a waiting plate. Other than the meat, the plate was empty. She didn't need any sides to distract her from what really mattered. Besides, demons didn't *eat* human food. Her type didn't eat flesh. Were all these rules necessary?

As she walked over to the round, wooden table by the large window spanning from top to bottom of the far wall, she caught a glimpse of her image in the oval shaped, full-length mirror across the room. She paused, plate in one hand, wine glass in the other. She wasn't acting like a demon spawned from Asmodeus, groomed to suck death-metal aura. She didn't look like one, either. A strange red hue circled the perimeter of her eyeballs. A sickly grey had taken over the creamy tone of her human face.

She snapped her gaze away from the mirror and stomped toward the table. As she set the plate and wine glass down and settled into a chair, she looked out at the street below. It was quite the view, nestled in the downtown core, the heart of the city. She loved to species watch, taking in the silly mannerisms of these humans.

She filled her glass from a decanter set on the table, watching the rich, red liquid reach legs down the inside of the glass. Setting it down, she picked up a steak knife and a fork. She stopped and stared at the plate.

A tiny claw of fear scratched up her throat again. She clenched her jaw. Was this a bad idea? Could she handle the wrath if it came down on her?

As she stared at the fillet, cooked to perfection, juices seeping from it onto the plate, an image crept from the crevice of her demon brain. A little girl in a filthy nightgown, clawing at fresh soil, the bright moon illuminating the hidden truth.

The stomach of her borrowed body grumbled, a loud guttural sound. Her mouth watered as saliva escaped the corners of her mouth. The hunger and the thirst had surmounted to a debilitating level. She could barely function.

She plunged the fork into the centre of the meat. She slid the blade across the fillet. Perching a large chunk on the prongs of the fork, she held it up and admired the moist fillet, dripping with red juices. She thrust the fork into her mouth and slid the chunk from the prongs. As she chewed, she closed her eyes and lost herself in the first bite of satisfaction.

After two more bites, she tossed the knife and fork onto the table and grabbed the remaining fillet with her hands. Shoving the perfectly cooked flesh into her mouth, she chomped and chewed crudely, swallowing back large pieces, gurgling on the juices as they slid down her chin.

It was over in a flash. She leaned back against the chair and stared at the empty plate, red juices settled in the middle.

Stunned, she sat in silence for several moments.

She reached for the glass and drank back the entire contents. The rich red coated the digesting meat. Her body settled. She didn't feel full, but she felt satisfied. For now.

Having no idea how long it would last, she poured herself another glass of red, and sipped it slowly as she relived the process of its curation.

Images of cutting into Drakkar Noir-doused Jake, butchering his body into pieces, floated through her thoughts. As the blood had trickled, her mouth had watered. She couldn't waste such precious life juice. So, she'd collected it. Simmered it on low over the stove, adding spices to turn it into a mulled wine of sorts.

She was a death metal demon, yes.

Something was *off*. It had been since two feedings ago. When she drank the life essence of *Sage,* the lead singer of Soiled Carcass. She'd lost control at her next feeding. The Carnal Assault front man. She had to tear herself away from him, only to lose control again later that night on Jake, her boy-toy treat. She couldn't take it any longer. One cut. That's all she'd eat. Then she'd get rid of the rest, she silently promised herself.

Then again, did it really matter how she consumed humans if the main outcome was that she did just that...consume them?

Who was she fooling? *He* had been *clear* about the rules.

Fear scraped an icy claw down her back. She had to resolve this before *he* found out.

As she sipped the red, watched the milling humans on the street below, and pondered the predicament she found herself in, dread stretched tendrils inside of her borrowed body.

This much power, this much freedom to morph into multiple beings, if that's what was happening, could become a problem. She knew it. Yet, she couldn't resist the pull.

She took a long swig of mulled life juice and willed all thoughts to leave her mind. Fingers of hunger gripped her stomach again. Tonight, she would feast, and she would drink. Surely a full stomach and a good night's sleep would put her in a place to deal with her predicament in the morning.

Demon Blood

A collage of photos smeared across the screen of the laptop, running hot and humming loud. Sage leaned over the table, looming close to the screen, rubbing his eyes.

What in the metal fuck was going on?

Sleep deprived, his mind whirling with images of a white face streaming with black ichor, he had to know if this image haunting him had any meaning.

He'd fired up his old laptop, hoping it still worked. The amount of heat coming off it was alarming as the searches he ran churned away for what seemed like forever before suddenly spilling results over the screen. After typing in various combinations of words trying to describe what he saw, the same image popped up several times. It was the eyes. And the mouth. Like black holes of evil. Dripping with some sort of viscous oil.

Every search he tried resulted in a similar face staring at him from the computer screen. Every description used the word *demon*.

How was he supposed to believe this?

A demon was an evil spirit or devil. They could possess a person. They could be forceful, fierce, and skillful performers of a specific activity.

Like sucking the life out of a metal man and taking him on a wild ride of hallucinations?

There were seven devils. Lucifer for pride, Mammon for greed, Asmodeus for lust, Leviathan for envy, Beelzebub for gluttony, Satan for wrath, and Belphegor for sloth.

Jesus metal god Christ.

He slammed the laptop shut and leaned back in the chair.

There was only one conclusion. He was going fucking crazy.

On the Edge

Elena shot back her third Fireball. The cinnamon-laced burn sizzled her throat and sweetened the back of her tongue. The opening act was still a half hour away. She'd started her routine earlier than usual tonight. She'd only been to Glowing Zombie once before and she loved the vibe even more this time.

After her Jake-fillet feast, she'd taken six full days off from consuming any form of human matter. When she woke from a twelve-hour coma-like sleep, the feeling of dread hung over her borrowed body, and her demon mind, like a storm cloud. She had gone too far. She knew it. If there was any chance her behaviour had gone unnoticed, she needed to clean up her act. Now.

After the six-day demon detox, consisting of long hours of sleep, holing up in the studio apartment, and plenty of natural water—yes, demon dehydration was a real thing—she'd felt like a new woman. Well, demon posing as a woman.

Hours before the show, she was itching to go. According to her feeding calendar, this was the proper night for a meal. She'd scoped out this place and the band ahead of time. She'd stuck to the schedule, almost, the only glitch that she showed up early. She'd consumed her first Fireball within minutes of walking through the door of the seedy joint.

She swivelled the high stool, turning toward the stage, and leaning back against the bar.

She liked this place. It had the perfect aroma of one part cheap booze, one part sweat, and one part human matter. Most of them, the humans, didn't know, or pretended not to, that floors, walls, counters, and every other exposed surface in a place like this, were coated with a nice layer of human matter. Oil from fingertips, sweat from glands, fecal matter clinging to unwashed hands, saliva dripping from glasses, and a plethora of other delights mixed together in a perfect human-matter cocktail, coating the entire place. Many public locations were like this, but *this* kind of place was the best to be if you enjoyed the aroma of such a cocktail as much as Elena did.

Feeling settled back into her demon persona and her borrowed rocker-chick body, she scanned the building crowd, ready for the show. She wished the opening act was over. She wanted to get to the part she came for. The main act. The heavy metal front man. Eager to be back home, a perfect execution of a feeding night under her belt, she sat and waited, anxiously.

"Another?" The bartender, young, early twenties, shoulder-length blond hair, leaned over the bar.

"Sure." Elena couldn't resist. She knew she should slow down, but her nerves were building. It was rare for her to be so *uncomposed.* She had to get a hold of it before the show started. She needed to find a place to keep her energy, her thirst, and her hunger on simmer until the right time to feed.

The bartender returned with her shot of Fireball. "First time seeing the band?" he asked. His blue eyes were too pure.

"Yeah." She shot back the cinnamon-fire liquid, hoping it would tame the lust heating her body.

"Holy Cross. They're good. Rough. Raw. Opening act, Pestilential Flesh. Never seen them. Heard they're better than the opener." His blond locks fell over his bare shoulders. His tight tank clung to his sinewy body.

Not as muscular as she liked them, yet he seeped a pureness that was hard for her to resist. Maybe he could be her distraction, until feeding time. Better to let the sexual desire build than lose control of her hunger or consume too much alcohol. Even aura-sucking demons had their limits.

She flirted with him, only releasing him when he had to attend to restless patrons. As she watched him pouring a pint of golden beer, a rumbling erupted from the stage. She swivelled in the chair, feeling like herself again. Hoping the opening act would entertain her enough to keep her distracted, she leaned back against the bar.

A guitar riff ripped through the room. Elena nodded to the electric strums. The lead singer, orange-red hair flowing down his back, leather-clad legs rippling with muscles, fingers adorned with metal rings, stomped across the stage, guitarist hovering behind him. His voice captivated the audience. It gripped her the moment it reached rough-tinged angelic fingers across the room, straight into her soul. Her demon being whirled with raw energy. Her mind blanked. All she could sense was the sound of the voice.

In a trance, she slipped from the stool and wove through the crowd. Droplets of beer and human liquids landed on her arms as she made her way to the front. She looked up at the front man. His hair whipped wildly, his auburn eyes searched the crowd, his voice hypnotized her. Hunger rumbled in the pit of her belly. Thirst scratched at the edges of her dry throat. Weakness weighed down her human body, and her demon soul. Fragments of images shimmered in her mind. A little girl in a filthy night gown in a graveyard. A figure looming up on a hill. A moon glowing bright.

She couldn't take it any longer.

She closed her eyes, tilted her head back, and raised her arms. The crowd stilled. The room darkened.

Her human body shuddered under the exertion. Her demon instincts flared a warning. Something wasn't right. She couldn't risk drawing this out.

She opened her mouth and breathed deeply.

The singer's mouth responded, opening. A stream of cosmic orange and red swirled from within him, shooting toward her, plunging into her open mouth, down the waiting cavern. Time stood still. The crowd blurred around her. The stream of aura boiled her blood, singed her insides, and electrified her senses.

Her body jolted. Her mouth snapped shut.

The singer fell to the stage.

She scanned the crowd with wild eyes, frantically grasping for her bearings.

A few concertgoers turned and looked at her. She spun and lunged for the back of the bar, pushing sweaty arms out of her way. When she reached the edge of the mob, she emerged, escaping from the tight-packed bodies and heavy, moist air. She stopped, steadied herself. The cute, blue-eyed bar-tender stood behind the bar, eyes fixated on the stage. Whatever was happening behind her, she needed to get out of here now.

She turned and bolted for the door, half walking, half jogging, not wanting to cause any suspicion. She reached the door, opened it, and stepped into a blast of icy air. The door slammed shut. She breathed in and closed her eyes. Her being settled, the whirling sensation halted. It was OK. She took one more breath, then opened her eyes.

A face loomed mere inches from her.

She gasped.

Onyx eyes, inches from her, stared her down, freezing her in place.

Her entire being stopped. Her breath, her thoughts, her motion halted.

It was *him.*

A barrage of images flooded her mind, flickering from one to the next like a lost-footage horror film. A cold, dark cemetery. A luminescent moon. Her younger self, cowering by a pile of soil. *Him.* Towering over her. The mere scent of him sending her limbs into tremors. His onyx eyes, icy daggers, piercing into her soul.

It couldn't be. She'd escaped his powerful grip so long ago. She'd broken the rules. Murder. Flesh eating. Blood drinking. And now *this.* She'd gone in too early and too eager for her feeding. Her hold on the crowd had been weak. She'd exposed herself as she'd fed right in front of them. The wrath she'd been waiting for would be unpleasant. The consequences of breaking the rules as an aura-sucking demon were...*painful.*

This. This was far worse than anything she could have imagined or expected.

He was something she'd prayed to the demon gods she'd never have to face again.

THE NEEDLE

S age bolted upright. Darkness cloaked his surroundings. Narrowing his eyes, he searched the crevices of the room, desperate to ground his mind.

Pain pricked the inner fold of his elbow. He extended his right arm. Panic shot through him, searing his veins, seizing his brain.

A syringe protruded from his flesh, the needle stuck straight into the soft underbelly of his arm.

No.

This can't be real.

As his vision adjusted, the outline of the room became clear. Four walls lined with broken people clutching needles. The red door. The chipped picture frame hanging crooked on the wall, the glass shattered across a photo of an old woman.

No.

How was it possible? How could he be here, in the exact place from three years ago. *Three fucking years.*

He yanked the syringe from his arm and threw it to the ground. It clanked across the filthy floor. Blood trickled from the hole it left behind, the one that had fed the poison straight into his vein. His arm shook as he stared at the crusted holes dotting his skin. A single tear burst from the corner of his bloodshot eye and dripped down his dirt-caked cheek.

This can't be real.

His scalp pulled tight as he concentrated hard, searching his memories, trying to make some sort of sense of his situation.

He remembered this place. His rock bottom. More than his rock bottom. The night he chose liquid relief over himself, his music, his bandmates...*life*. He'd crawled into the corner of this room of desperation, joining the other lost souls who'd given in. As the needle pierced his skin, the second the potent fluid dripped from the tip into his vein, he knew something was wrong. The toxic liquid had shot through his veins in an instant, blasting his heart and turning his skin blue. He'd lost all control. The days, hours, minutes, leading up to this very moment were a blur of images. How many hits had he taken? How many substances had he indulged in? How had he gotten to this dank room dripping with desperation? Where had he gotten the poison running through his veins now?

The memory that simmered in the back of his brain now told him that he couldn't answer any of these questions.

He closed his eyes and willed the world spinning around him to disintegrate. It couldn't be.

When he'd woken in the hospital, his bandmates hovering around his bed, he'd sworn he'd never get to this place again.

This couldn't be. It made no sense. Three years. Two albums. A six-month tour. No drugs.

The powder on his glass table in his apartment flashed through his thoughts. The night after the raven-haired woman looked into his eyes from the crowd below. The night the depletion started and everything slid downwards.

How much of the last few weeks could he remember clearly? Was he really here right now.

His eyes popped open. He looked around. Men, women, weakened by the drugs pumping through their veins, exhausted from the constant hunt for the substances they couldn't survive without, curled into themselves, rocked back and forth, and lay sprawled on the floor. Panic clawed up his throat. His brain buzzed. He grabbed tangled, sweat-drenched locks of his hair, pulling them hard, hands trembling, shoulders shaking.

He looked across the room at the old woman peering through the shattered glass. Her face paled as it aged. Her eyes spun into black orbs, dark ichor dripped down her cheeks, and darkness took over her thin mouth as it formed a circle and opened, revealing a deep cavern.

Sage shook his head, squeezed his eyes shut and lowered his forehead to his knees. Ice-cold air swirled around him, scratching nails down his arms.

He screamed.

The room shook.

The cold air vanished.

He opened his eyes. Upright in his bed, clutching sweat-drenched sheets in his trembling hands, he looked around his apartment. It was quiet. No photo of an old woman. No supernatural being with ichor dripping from her eyes. No needle. It was him and only him.

Flinging the bed covers aside, he pulled on a pair of sweatpants, trudged over to the refrigerator, and pulled out a bottle of Rolling Rock. The cheesy *Kiss* bottle opener that Turbo had bought him as a gag gift didn't even elicit a slight chuckle as he yanked the cap off the bottle. He chugged half the beer then walked over to the table by the big window. The moon cast an unworldly silver glow over the apartment. His muscular weight heavy against the creaky wooden chair, he set the bottle on the table and opened the laptop.

Still running hot and loud, he hoped it would last for another round of fucked-up research.

Images of white faces dripping in black sludge bombarded him. He closed them all, then launched another round of searches, this time looking for answers to what must be dreams or hallucinations but seemed to be so real he felt like he was living them.

After opening a second bottle of Rolling Rock and pacing the room for what felt like forever while waiting for the computer to give him some answers, he stared at the bright computer screen glowing through the dark room.

Delusional disorder. A person could actually believe in an alternate reality. Reality was *not* real. *Schizophrenia.* Symptoms included hallucinations and delusions. *Demonic Possession* also resulted in the same symptoms. People with psychotic disorders could have the delusional belief that evil or demons possessed them.

Had he imagined it all? Did the raven-haired rocker chick exist? Or had he hallucinated her entire existence. But Dagger had seen her. Although, how could he be sure they'd seen the *same* woman?

He ran his hands wildly through his tangled hair and over his sweat-coated face. Tilting the bottle to his lips, he chugged back the rest of the beer.

He was losing his fucking mind.

Mordis

Elena was prepared to face *them*. The leaders of her world where demons of various permutations were birthed. She wasn't prepared to face *him*. Mordis, the one who had saved her life, gave her a new chance, *created her*. She knew he'd kept tabs on her, tracking her whereabouts from time to time, and because he had given her to them, he still had claim over her at his very whim. She took a few steps back, the heels of her boots clicking against the pavement.

Mordis followed her steps, keeping the gap between them tight. Bass thrummed through the door behind her. She wondered if she could slip back through and lose him in the crowd.

His eyes, pupils rimmed with a red glow, pierced into her soul, holding her captive. "My dear *Elena,* you have been ill behaved."

She detested the sly emphasis he placed on her name. She licked her lips and swallowed a dribble of saliva down the dry scales of her parched throat. Her voice came out weaker than she wanted it to be. "I stuck to the feeding schedule and type. Once a week. Front men for heavy metal bands. I've still got several months here."

"Yes, Elena, your *feeding* habits have been...on par. Your *other* behaviours have not." Mordis raised a raven eyebrow, stretching the smooth, olive skin over his right eye. "The ones of a rather sexual nature."

"There aren't any rules about interacting with humans for sexual gratification." She pulled her cherry lips into a thin line. *Except that you shouldn't murder your late-night treat and then eat him.*

"No, there aren't. But a certain dark-haired gentlemen, a Jake Holt, vanished after you took him home the other night. After your feeding at Metal Panther." Mordis turned and fluttered his thin fingers. "Poof. Gone. Vaporized into thin air."

"He left my place fine." Cellophane-wrapped packages of carefully carved cutlets shimmered through her mind. Would he buy it? Would he demand to see her apartment? Not that he needed permission to do so.

Mordis walked toward her, staring her down. His face, inches from hers, he whispered hot, spicy breath across her nose. "Are you sure about that?" He hovered.

Elena froze, willing her limbs not to quiver and resisting the desire to swallow. "Yes."

Mordis turned, raising his hands in the air. "Very well. We will simply have to keep an eye out for him. I suppose he's slipped through the cracks of our intel."

They both knew how unlikely that was. What would she do? Her freezer was packed with every cut of Jake that you could imagine.

"Tell me, are you well?"

She took several more steps backward, nearing the door. Electric guitar wails vibrated behind her.

She forced confidence into her voice. "Why do you ask?"

"We have a special bond, you and I. Given the nature of our relationship. I can *feel it* when you aren't whole. Lately, I sense you are slipping away."

"I'm fine." She bit back the urge to let her feelings flow. He had saved her life, after all, he must care, at least somewhat.

He approached her, scooping her chin into his soft palm. "I *can* trust you, can't I?"

The icy night air scraped her face. The stars spun into shimmering streaks of silver, blending with the midnight sky. Elena closed her eyes and fought down a wave of nausea. When she opened her glitter-dusted lids, she was in her apartment, kneeling on the floor.

Mordis hovered over her, his red-rimmed pupils glowing. "If you have told me the truth, then I apologize in advance. Something inside of me is telling me to *verify* this tale you have spun."

Elena sat down on the floor and curled her legs into her chest. She silently begged for some way out of this. He wouldn't be convinced easily.

He paused halfway to the kitchen and glared at her with his hot, red eyes. "You *know* we can't have *new* demons running around killing anyone they want to. Until you learn how to be discreet, we can't have the humans aware. It would be exorcism hell." He spun and strode over to the kitchen.

New. She felt like she'd been a demon forever. She'd just turned six-hundred-and-sixty-six, for fuck's sake.

Doors crashed and cupboards slammed as he scoured the apartment. Hot fear seared her insides. Chunks of plastic-wrapped human flesh flashed through her mind. He halted in front of the refrigerator. It hummed softly through the thick silence.

He raised his arm, his hand paused in front of the handle. An audible sniff prickled her ears as he took a deep breath, exploring the odours behind the door. His hand shot up. He yanked the freezer open. Human fillets fell around his boots, hitting the floor with loud thuds.

This is it.

Elena buried her face in her hands and clenched her jaw. She needed to find the strength to fight the wrath of her creator.

A woosh jolted her. Mordis' face nearly touching hers, red glowed from the entire surface of both his eyes.

"This is human." He thrust a plastic-wrapped Jake steak at her.

She swallowed, her mind racing, trying to find the right words.

He leaned closer, then took a long whiff of her.

"You've fed. On human flesh." He stood, dropped the meat with a loud clank. He waved his arm across the room. A red shimmer sprinkled over the space.

Elena stared at the open freezer, now empty. Mordis balled his fist. He crouched and breathed heavily into her face. Sweat trickled down her back. Her heart thrummed against her ribcage.

His red, glowing eyes bored into hers. She tried to swallow, but no moisture came.

His fist moved dangerously close to her. He unfurled his fingers and grazed her face with his trembling fingertips.

"Elena. You must not break the rules. After all I have done for you…" His expression softened for a brief moment, the red fading from his eyes. The volume in his voice shocked her with his final words. "The rules were to protect you."

Something glimmered in his eyes, perhaps a droplet of love.

She swallowed back a ball of emotion surging up her throat.

"It's awoken within you. It's too late. I can't protect you any longer." Cold washed over his face, taking every drop of feeling with it. "You get one final chance."

With a swift *poof*, he was gone, leaving Elena in a swirl of orange-red mist.

Investigation

The metal community was a tight one. Despite the rough image they had, they were a caring bunch. It had been easy for Sage to reach out to all the local bands. Many of them had supported Soiled Carcass' album launch, playing at shows along their tour route. They were all eager to hear how the tour was going and to shoot the shit. When Sage asked them about their recent shows, a pattern emerged.

He walked up to the fire engine red refrigerator humming away in the corner of the kitchen and opened the door. He pulled out a bottle of Rolling Rock and grabbed his *Kiss* bottle opener off the counter. He stared at the band logo, faces painted white and black like sinister cats, and shook his head. The beer hissed as he pulled the cap off. The bubbles soothed his throat as he took a long swig.

His depletion was getting worse. The visions were out of control. He was afraid to go to sleep, not wanting to feel the sheer terror of reliving his past. Unable to face the piercing of the needle into his arm the night he nearly died. Every time he relived it, it was more than a dream or a vision. It was real. It was like he was there, living every gut-wrenching moment over again. Her face would appear, in the picture frame, snapping him back to the present moment. Sometimes it was her and only her that took him on a night-terror ride, hovering over him, her hundred-year-old face dripping with black evil, plastered over his ceiling.

It had been eight days since he'd spotted the raven-haired woman at Metal Panther when Dagger fell to his knees.

The band meeting the next day went well. Turbo apologized. He took a foot off the party pedal after that, having a good time, but maintaining his ability to slam out killer drumbeats night after night. They'd polished off three more shows. By the end of the last one, Sage could barely move his limbs. He'd crumpled with relief and thanked the metal gods when he realized they had a full week off. They had a couple more weeks left on the tour. He would give anything to finish it off strong.

He'd holed up in his apartment, convinced he could replenish his energy. As the visions heightened, his sleep deprivation skyrocketed and his desperation swelled. He couldn't shake the instinct swelling in his gut that the raven-haired woman had something to with all the fucked-up shit that was happening to him. Seeing the lead singer of Carnal Assault fall to the stage at the very moment she was in the crowd could not have been a coincidence. And the singer, Dagger, had *seen* the woman right after crumpling to the stage. Just like Sage had.

The state he was in paired with the *coincidental as fuck* happenings had spawned his need to investigate further, and his onslaught of catching up with the other bands.

Beer in hand, he walked over to the table perched by a huge window, overlooking the street below. He loved to people watch from here, where no one knew he was looking. People in their natural habitat, surrounded by tall glass buildings and shops, fascinated him.

He set the bottle of beer on the table, pulled out a chair, and sat. He looked over the open notebook, reviewing the timeline he'd sketched out as he'd talked to each band.

Locust Lust, Dominion Day, Rage of Fire, Rotted Teeth—they'd all had smooth gigs over the last few weeks. Nothing unusual. The normal, status-quo metal scene.

Careening Corpse, Death Animal, Savage Seer, and *Ten Steps to Hell*—they had expressed an entirely different experience. The story was the same every time. The last few weeks had been smooth. But if they looked back over the last few months, which each of them did when Sage inquired about anything *unusual* during a show, their stories aligned. Over the last few months, they'd pulled off their gigs without the tiniest snag. Except one show. They all had one show where something extremely strange had occurred. Part way through their performance, their lead singer had frozen, mid wail. It was the weirdest thing. Then, suddenly, the singer fell to their knees, landing on the stage in some sort of crumpled form. In every case, one or more of the band members had approached the singer, keeping the song going, to determine if they were all right. In every case, the lead singer would come to when spoken to, stand shakily, get his bearings, belt out the next note, then finish off the show. In every case, the lead singer was less eager to party it up back-stage after, looking pale and depleted. Every account was from a performance right here, in his beloved city. Only one of the singers, from Ten Steps to Hell, remembered seeing the raven-haired woman.

Yes, they all had an image to keep.

Yet, Sage had always found the members of the metal community grounded, open, honest. They were a supportive bunch. They weren't afraid to talk to each other.

None of them found it unusual for Sage to call up and ask how they were doing. None of them were shy about sharing the strange experience. They knew it would be kept between them.

Sage took a long pull on the beer and leaned back into the chair. It crackled under his muscular weight.

What was he going to do? It couldn't possibly be a coincidence that several lead singers had undergone a near identical experience to his own, all in a matter of months. And all in the same city.

They all lived the same wild lifestyle. They were all tempted by the drugs and alcohol flying from open hands after every show. They all lived hard on and off stage, and sometimes between shows. For most of them, once they tasted it, they craved more. It was *human* to enjoy the high so much that resisting it became impossible.

He shook his head. *No.* This couldn't be a coincidence. Hell, he'd even gone back to Bad Idol and questioned the staff. There was one bartender, Johnny, who remembered her. He said he'd gone home with her but didn't have a clear recollection of where she lived. Guess he'd hit the shots hard after his shift ended. *Elena.* That was her name, according to him.

If he shared his theory with his fellow metal men, what would they say?

He sounded crazy. To himself. He would definitely sound nuts to anyone else if he shared this with them.

He sighed and took another long pull from the beer. Looking out the window, he scanned the street, watching the people walk by, some in a hurry, some taking their time.

Something caught his eye. He stood and walked to the window.

It was her.

Black spikes of hair. Leather jacket concealing her arms. Scarf wrapped around her neck, hiding half her face. He could only see her side profile, yet he was sure it was her. The cherry-lipped woman with the dark eyes, staring at him from the dance floor as he wailed his metal god lyrics to the crowd. She walked past the window. He ran across the room, flung the door open, and bolted down the hallway.

He ran by the elevator—it would be too slow—and into the stairwell. Taking the stairs two at a time, he made it down the four flights at top speed. Lunging through the front doors of the building, he slid to a stop on the walkway. He looked in the direction she'd been walking. He frantically examined each person, searching for pale skin, raven spikes, tattoos. She was gone. Or she'd never been there.

He ran his fingers through his hair. He was losing his grip, and for a metal god, it wasn't cool.

Morning After

A soft yellow glow filtered through the cream-coloured curtains fluttering in the crisp breeze. Elena opened her eyes and scanned the room. She was in bed. In her apartment. Thoughts of the evening trailed through her mind.

She could still feel the softness of Mordis' hand on her chin. She could still hear his words of warning. *You get one final chance.*

Fucking Mordis. He was the one who had saved her. Created her. She *should* be thankful. She couldn't help but wish she was free of his control.

The image of the young girl in the graveyard grew vivid in her brain. The fragments of memories floating in the crevices of her demon mind ever since her hunger pains had started now clicked together, forming a perfect picture.

Mordis had found her under the glow of the florescent moon, crouched over a grave, moist soil clinging to her ragged nails as she dug into a plot marked Mary Ann Beacham. He'd taken pity on her. She was only six. She had no recollection of how she'd gotten out of the orphanage and into the cemetery. She couldn't comprehend why she was digging with her hands into a place where the dead rested.

The orphanage didn't know what to do with her. Mordis took her in. He said he understood the effects of trauma on a young child, and that he could help her find her way. The orphanage didn't protest. Elena could still see the relief on the faces of the young women who cared for the orphans as she left the building, one tiny bag of clothes in one hand, and Mordis' hand in her other.

She never did understand her strange cravings and tendencies. He'd told her that her soul was evil, there was nothing wrong with that, and she could choose a number of manifestations for her being.

All she'd wanted was to be human and to be near other humans. He'd guided her in the way of the demon. A demon could take on any human form, borrow any body they wanted to. They could even thrive without killing any humans, by perfecting their skills of possession and feeding on auras.

She stretched her arms over her head and found the floor with her bare feet. She padded across the room and stood in front of the fridge, humming softly.

Maybe everything that happened last night had only been a nightmare. She opened the freezer. An emptiness filled her belly. Every morsel of human meat, Jake cutlets, boy-toy flesh, was gone. Hunger swelled in her gut.

She'd sucked the aura of a human that wasn't her assigned type until the life left his body. *Strike one.*

She'd eaten his flesh, carved into a beautiful steak. *Strike two.*

She'd fed in front of a room full of witnesses. *Strike three.*

Mordis said she had one more chance. Why?

Grumbling erupted in her gut. The cold of the empty freezer seeped over her face. Desperation took hold of her.

What was she going to do?

She wanted to remain a demon. She loved being a demon. It was one of the closest things to human that an evil supernatural soul could be. She'd worked hard to perfect her ability to borrow a body and completely suppress the human within without harm. She fed off auras to thrive.

No harm. No foul.

Over the years, every jagged image of her young past had become more and more fragmented. The memories had been broken and buried deep into the recesses of her demon mind. Whatever she had been was gone. Why had everything resurfaced now?

Staring at the cold, empty space where the packages of perfectly butchered meat had been, she wondered if her past was now hunting her down.

Why had Mordis found her hovering over a grave, soil caking her nails? How had she known the technique of butchering a human body? Why was she craving human flesh and blood after a particularly luscious metal-god-aura feeding?

She ran her hand down her face and over the grotesque, sickly grey contours that the milky-smooth skin of her human face had morphed into. She closed her eyes and pictured the red, glowing rings around the white spheres that kept getting brighter every time she looked in the mirror.

Triple Header

It was a triple header. *Satan's Slut. Cranial Crave.* And the headliner, *Primal Pulse.* The Velvet Owl was famous for their low cover charge and three-band nights.

If the raven-haired, tattooed, pale woman Sage had seen from the stage the night his manic metal energy dipped lower than ever before was indeed somehow responsible for his depletion, and if she was indeed on some sort of metal front men *depletion* rampage, then this would be the night that she would strike. The triple header was the most *metal* of all the shows of the evening within her apparent striking zone, and it was on the night of her apparent depletion schedule, according to the intel he'd gathered.

He liked this place. It was dark, yet a certain warmth ebbed from the pot lighting lining the perimeter of the low ceiling. He'd played many shows here over the years.

As he approached the bar, looking for a corner to launch his stakeout, a young bartender with curly blonde hair bouncing over her shoulders and grazing her plump breasts bolted to the counter. "Look what the cat drug in. Didn't see you on the lineup tonight."

"Just a spectator."

"Your usual?" She fluttered her eyelashes, golden shimmer sparkled under the light casting an angelic glow over her glossy hair.

Sherry was anything but angelic.

"Yeah. And get one for yourself." He slipped several bills into her hand. "And I'd like to keep it on the down low that I'm here tonight."

Sherry blushed as she eyed the money. She didn't shy away from the offer. Off she bounced to get his drink.

Rumbles from the stage warned of the start of the show. Sage scanned the bar and moved to the far end, a darker corner where he could keep to himself.

Moments later, he was settled on a rickety chair, his broad shoulders leaning against the chipped wall. Sherry appeared with two drinks. Without a word, she nodded at him and they shot back the Jack Daniel's in a silent toast.

A swirl of colours bathed the stage. A savage drumbeat herded the crowd toward the stage. The Satan's Slut front man jumped to the front of the stage, yanked the mic from its stand and belted out the opening words to the first track without a breath.

Dan. His name was Dan. He looked like a feral animal left to fend on the streets. He was the first one to help out a fellow metal head in need.

If Sage was right, Dan would be safe from the strange rocker woman. She would wait until the headliner before making her move. He scanned the bar again, still no sign of her. In a silent prayer, he pleaded with the metal gods that he'd picked the right show.

As he watched Dan flailing across the stage, he wondered if he should warn the lead singer of Primal Pulse.

Then he almost laughed out loud as he shook his head. What would he say? There's a rock chick going to metal shows and magically stealing the energy from lead singers? They'd think he was crazy. They'd shake their heads in embarrassment, thinking that drugs and booze had taken the mind of another one in their metal community.

A nervous energy usually saved for the pre-show trickled through his veins. He signalled Sherry to bring another drink. One more. Calm the nerves. Then he'd keep his eyes focused on the crowd and the patrons lining the bar.

As soon as he spotted the raven-haired woman, and he was sure he would, he'd slide up beside her and quietly confront her. He'd get to the bottom of this. Find some sort of explanation for his extreme depletion and the fucked-up visions that plagued him every night.

He wasn't the cause of his exhaustion. She was. Somehow, he *knew it*. Just as he knew that the night terrors were linked to whatever she'd done to him that night four weeks ago.

He knew what he'd seen. What he'd *felt*. And it was all linked to this mysterious, tattooed, raven-haired woman.

Metal Saviour

A haze trickled its cloudy fingers over the basement bar. The purple-and-blue lights bathing the stage swirled in a fuzzy cosmic glow. Elena blinked hard, then narrowed her eyes, trying to bring the lead singer into focus.

Was this still the opening act?

The face of the metal man remained a blurry sphere. She had no idea who he was.

Twisting in her chair, she scanned the bar. Two empty shot glasses stuck to the counter directly in front of her. How long had she been sitting here? Had she had more than two shots of Fireball? She wrenched her brain, but her mind was a vacant tunnel.

A boyish bartender slid up to the counter. He was exactly her type. "Another?" He winked.

She swallowed, sat up straight, looked him in the eye. "Sure."

She needed to get her act together. This confused state of haze was foreign. She was Elena. Demon of darkness spawned from lust. Eater of death metal gods. What *the fuck* was happening to her?

A growl erupted in the bowels of her belly, vibrating her body. The desert in her throat scratched claws down the back of her tongue and ripped at her esophagus.

The week flashed before her eyes. Mordis had taken her Jake cutlets. He'd given her *one more* chance. She'd devoured nothing inappropriate. No flesh. No blood. Sleep had consumed her at an early evening hour and pulled her late into the next morning. All her focus had been on making it to the next feeding day.

Now, here she was, ready to redeem herself. Along with the hunger and thirst, a heavy exhaustion pulled her down.

The bartender returned. "For you, hot stuff." He set two shots on the counter. "One for you, one for me. My treat."

Hot stuff. Did she look better than she felt?

She smiled, lifted the glass in a toast, and shot back the Fireball.

Cinnamon and spice burned her throat, soothing it, coating it, weaving a numbness through her limbs.

"Who's the band?" She risked revealing how out of it she was. If he was as nice as he appeared, he would overlook it.

"Cranial Crave." He smiled. "Seen them before?"

"No." *Had she? Was the Cranial Crave lead singer her targeted meal?*

"They're good. Better than the main act. But don't tell anyone I said so." He winked again then turned to tend to a rowdy bunch at the end of the bar.

Weariness ravaged her insides. Hunger growled again, more fierce than before.

She turned and looked up at the stage. The front man stood tall. Long locks of raven hair whipped around his smooth face. His eyes, orbs of darkness, scanned the room. His voice wove through the space, pure, strong, the perfect amount of rawness tingling its edges.

Elena's hunger grew wild, clawing up her entire body, forcing her mouth to widen, excreting droplets of saliva down the corners of her lips. Her body stood. She had no control.

As she wove through the wild crowd elbows and arms bounced off her, screams piercing her ears. In a trance, she didn't flinch, feel, or hear. The only thing that mattered was the hunger.

At the lip of the stage, Elena tilted her head back and her mouth widened. The metal god jolted. His head flung forward. His lips responded to her demon call, stretching wide, forming a perfect circle. A blood-orange glow pulsed over the stage and the crowd as a fluorescent stream shimmered from him to her. Elena drank and drank, one massive unending gulp. Her hunger continued. It refused to ease.

The metal god dropped to his knees. The mic fell from his hand, hitting the floor. Whining feedback echoed through the room. The crowd turned as one being and stared at the singer. Their eyes followed the cosmic stream, landing on the tattooed, raven-haired rock chick at the other end.

"Her! It's her." A curvaceous woman with backcombed bleached-blonde hair pointed at Elena.

The crowd, like a single being, lunged, knocking Elena from her feeding frenzy.

Her shoulder hit the ground first, followed by the back of her head. Her silver-streaked eyelids fluttered. Dozens of angry eyes loomed over her. A droplet of sweat leaped from the mascara-smeared face of the blonde woman and landed on Elena's cheek.

The room blurred.

"Mordis..." the word, barely a whisper, escaped her lips.

Strong arms slid underneath her, one hooked under her knees, the other cradled her back. She was lifted. She didn't fight. She couldn't.

The heat of the space dulled. The odour of sweat and cheap booze faded. Crisp air hit her face. Fresh rain infused her nostrils, landing on her skin in soft droplets. She opened her eyes.

She knew this face staring down at her. Those eyes.

"Relax. You're safe."

That voice.

Sage.

Electric Passion

P anic soared through Elena's veins. Her borrowed heart thrummed, threatening to crack her ribcage. She was the Metal Demon. She was supposed to be powerful and *in control*. She wasn't supposed to be the weak fucking damsel in distress.

With every last bit of strength she had within her, she tried to wrench herself from Sage's arms—his strong, safe, muscular hold. Her body shuddered and she collapsed even heavier into his grasp.

He didn't break his stride as he looked down at her. Glossy locks of blond fluttered over his emerald eyes. "Relax. I won't hurt you."

That voice.

She'd drank in many metal god voices. None of them had a hold on her like his.

Sage stopped and set her feet onto the pavement. He leaned her upper body against his and wrapped his arm around her, pulling her close. His muscles rippled against her body as he manoeuvred his free arm and held her tightly with the other. He smelled like the forest after a fresh rain.

What the metal fuck was wrong with her?

She was supposed to desire his specific type of human form. But only to *feed*. She wasn't supposed to be attracted to him. Her bartender boy toys were for that.

And this...this wave of tingles surging through her body, circling into the vortex of her sexual pot, this was more than physical desire.

She sunk into a plush cushion. Fluttering her eyelids, she could make out the outline of some sort of truck. She was in the back seat.

Sage's hot breath grazed her face as he sat down next to her and leaned in close. "Are you OK?"

Emotion paralyzed her as she tried to move her lips. His fresh-rain scent, the support of his muscular arm still around her, his death metal essence, it was too much. She nodded, her eyes locked on his.

Whatever was happening, it broke all the rules of her demon world.

Before she could breathe another breath, his lips were on hers. She melted under his dominance. A trace of Jack Daniel's on his lips tantalized her tongue.

She lost all control.

His hands, strong yet soft, tore her shirt, exposing her breasts. His touch hardened her nipples despite the heat of the tight space. With his fingers and his tongue, he explored her.

She didn't fight. She wasn't herself. She was lost in waves of tingling heat.

As he gripped her pleather pants and slid them down her legs, she arched her back, silently permitting him to embark on a journey neither of them had ever experienced.

As he lowered his hot, muscular body against hers, she wrapped her bare legs around his torso. As this human man, only a god on stage with a voice from heaven, yet human in flesh and bone, entered her, the evil force from another world, an explosion of colour, heat, and electric pulses overtook her.

She was no longer present on the earth.

A cosmic journey took her on a wild ride of physical lust and raw emotion. When she landed, she lay breathless in his arms, sweat trickling down her face and body.

He looked at her with shock and confusion. As he untangled himself from her body, both of them glistening with sweat, he said, "I don't know what happened."

Elena pulled herself to sitting and wrapped her arms around her legs. "That makes two of us."

Aftermath

The silver glimmer brushing Elena's eyelids sparkled under the soft glow of the overhead light in the cab of Sage's truck.

"What just happened?" Anger tinged Sage's voice as he roughly pulled his jeans over his legs. He paused to look at her, his emerald eyes still entrancing, the muscles clenching over his bare chest. "That wasn't...that was...what *was* that?"

"I don't know." Elena pulled her pleather pants over her legs and shuffled them over her exposed curves.

"No. I don't buy it. You hypnotized me." He pulled his shirt over his head. A white skull stretched across his chest as he yanked it down.

"No. I didn't. I'm not supposed to..." She bit her lip and cupped her palms over her breasts as she searched for her shirt.

He sighed and sat back against the seat, running his hands through his luscious hair. "Bad Idol. Four weeks ago. My show.

You were there." He turned his neck, finding her eyes with his. "You did something to me."

She slid her arms into the sleeves of her shirt and looked down in dismay at the ripped material, her breasts hanging free.

"I'm sorry. I don't know what came over me." His cheeks flushed.

Embarrassed. A metal god embarrassed.

"It's OK." She pulled her leather jacket on and zipped it up, caging her breasts.

"You did something to me." He spoke softer now, the anger dissipating.

"I..." She wanted to be honest. Why? She didn't know. The repercussions were too severe. "What could I have possibly done?"

He's human. He only knows human ways.

"Yeah. I get it. I sound crazy. How could *you* deplete my energy without so much as touching me? But then I saw you. Again. Metal Panther. A week later. The same thing happened to the lead singer of Carnal Assault. You were there. It was worse with him. You ran."

Flashes of the last few weeks burst through her mind. Feeding on Sage. Feeding on the front man of Carnal Assault and going too far. Drinking too much metal god aura from the singer of Pestilential Flesh at the Glowing Zombie. The hunger. The urges. Tonight. Feeding before the main act. Not being able to stop. The blood-orange drip of the metal god's essence something more incredible than she'd ever tasted.

The crowd. Hitting the ground.

Sage's arms around her.

Her loins tingled now. A luscious warmth washed through her as she looked into his eyes.

"Why?" She licked the cherry lipstick clinging to her upper lip.

"Why what?"

"Why did you help me?"

He rested his forehead on his palms. "No idea. The crowd turned on you. My instincts told me to help." He raised his head again. "I felt *pulled* to you." His gaze, now serious, searched deep into her soul. "I don't understand any of this."

He wasn't evil like her. He wanted answers.

"I..." She swallowed, closing her eyes. "I'm not like anyone you know."

"No shit."

"I..." She could see her lips moving, forming the words, telling him she was a demon sent to suck his soul.

Her hand shot out and yanked the door beside her open. Cold air burst into the hot cab.

He grabbed her arm as she started to slip from the truck. "What are you?"

"I can't." She tried to pull free, but he tightened his grip. He took a hard hold on her arms, pulling her back into the truck and pushing her against the seat. "You're not going anywhere. Not without giving me answers." The veins in his neck pulsed. His emerald eyes bored into her soul.

Droplets of sweat trickled over his arm, dripping onto hers. Wisps of white smoke swirled through the cab as her flesh sizzled.

He yanked his arm back. "What the fuck?"

Elena's mind whirled. Hot pokers seared her skin. She was losing control. Pam lunged from her box and thrust herself through her stolen body. Pam's voice escaped from her own lips before Elena could stop it. "Please. Help me. She has me."

Sage stared in shock.

Elena shook her head. She closed her eyes, summoned every ounce of her demon power, and raised her hands toward the roof of the cab. She slammed *fucking Pam* hard into her box. Pam's soul went limp. Elena opened her eyes and looked across the cab at Sage as her body rose from the seat and she hovered in the small space, looming close to him. His face went pale. Terror washed over his eyes.

Her demon blood boiled. Humans didn't control her. She was a demon of darkness. It was the other way around.

Her cherry lips parted. Her inner force swelled. A stream of blood-orange light shot from her mouth and forced him against the window. His head slammed back against the glass. It crackled into a ragged spider web. He choked as his hands clawed at his neck.

Pressing her lips together, she halted her attack.

He slumped down against the seat. He pulled his long hair from his face and whispered, "What the *hell* are you? You're *not* human. Some kind of fucking evil?"

Elena's true voice rumbled through her borrowed body, like something from the depths of hell. "Stay away from me."

She flung the door open and ran into the dark of night, cold air clawing at her cheeks.

If Sage confronted her again, she'd have to kill him.

Accused

A cold wind gushed through the sunbathed apartment. Elena jolted upright in bed. Her eyes darted around. She froze. *Mordis.*

The red rimming Mordis' eyes glowed. He crossed his arms, his legs in a wide stance, his lips forming a scowl. "You're out of control, *Elena.*"

She blinked several times as she wiped the crusts of sleep from her eyes. *What the fuck?*

A barrage of images bombarded her, reminding her of her actions the night before. She'd fed. The hunger had been *consuming.* She didn't wait for the main act. She sucked a sub-par metal man nearly dry of his essence. Angry faces pulsed in her mind. *Sage. Oh my metal god, Sage.* Heat rose through her body as droplets of sweat trickled down her neck.

Mordis took several deliberate steps, halting to loom over her. "You have a feeding type. You are not to cohort with them. It's not difficult." His venomous words stung her ears.

She cringed. How in the flying guitar riff did he know about her sexual encounter?

"And he was one on which you fed. You are drawing attention. You do remember what happened the last time you did that, don't you?"

The exorcism. It had been painful. Worse, it had been embarrassing how she'd been careless and let herself be revealed. Her back arched as she relived the hot pokers of pain that had seared her insides. The remnants of shame clenched her gut.

She nodded, pressing her lips into a thin line.

"It seems you've been rather indulgent. Your feasting lingers. You killed a human. You ate flesh. Now you are sexually ravishing the death metal man, the type you have been assigned to feed upon, and only feed upon, nothing more." He leaned closer. His hot copper breath tingled her nostrils. "Punishment."

She shivered.

"It was an accident." Heat swelled in her belly. "I'm too hungry. I'm not allowed enough feedings. It's thrown me off, I can't stop when I start to feed." She attempted a pathetic expression.

"Enough acting. You are naive. That is not the problem. Your true being has been awakened."

What? She was a demon. A death metal demon. A specific supernatural breed that allowed her to be as close to human as possible with her evil soul.

She licked her dry lips, her tongue catching on a remnant of cherry lipstick. "I don't understand."

"You will." A flash of light left Elena alone, surrounded by a glittering glow.

Grave Digger

The cold air of the night bit at Elena's cheeks. At high volume, the moon bathed the grassy hill upon which she perched. Her knees bent, her body in a low squat, she looked down at her filthy hands caked in rich soil.

Her stomach roiled as she stared at the ground. A hole opened where fresh soil had been pulled out, forming a mound beside a rectangular plot. A headstone, glossy under the moonlight, declared this to be the resting place of Mary Ann Beacham.

Her hands twitched as Elena shook her head and stood. What was she doing here? How could this be?

She examined her soiled white nightgown and her tiny feet. Shaking the dirt from her fingers, she stretched them out, her hands minuscule. Grabbing a strand of her hair, she pulled it out in front of her. Blonde. Long. Curly.

She was six years old again.

Her head jolted at a shuffling from the top of the hill. A figure stood, looking down at her. Onyx eyes rimmed with red glowed. Ice chilled her.

Mordis. The night he'd found her and saved her from strange cravings and a life that terrified her.

She blinked. The moon shimmered, fading away, turning into rays of sunlight dribbling lazily through the white curtains fluttering over the window.

She was sitting at the table in the one-room apartment.

What had happened?

An image? A flashback? She didn't know.

Mordis' words pulsed in her mind. *Your true being has been awakened. You will understand.*

After uttering those words and vanishing into a glitter-laced cloud, he'd stopped appearing. It was as if he'd abandoned her.

Images rose up from the recesses of her demon mind. The taste of fresh flesh on the back of her tongue. Blood dripping down her chin. Looking down into a grave, limbs torn from a body half exposed from a mad excavation.

What had she been when Mordis found her? He'd led her, taught her, shaped her into something that could survive in a human world despite her evil core. All these years she'd thought she was a supernatural force tinged with darkness, living as close to humans as possible. She'd eagerly taken on the demon form that he'd transformed her into, believing it was her true nature.

Everything had gone smoothly. Only once had she strayed from her destiny. She'd gone too far. She'd nearly been exorcised. Until Mordis had saved her.

She'd redeemed herself. Things had been on track. Until she'd fed on Sage. Had he awakened something within her? Her need to feast on a meal type outside her realm. A need for flesh and blood. A lustful craving beyond anything she'd ever felt.

Was she wrong about who she truly was?

The sun bathed the apartment in a soft golden glow. Like Sage's luscious hair.

She shook her head. What was wrong with her? She was losing her grip. Her *control*. She was a demon grown from the seed of Asmodeus. The drinker of death metal aura. She'd be damned if she would let go of what was rightly hers. Yet, she felt powerless. She'd killed. She'd feasted upon human flesh. She'd drank human blood. Was her true nature something horrible and grisly? She gagged at the wet, metallic taste clinging to the back of her throat.

The palm of her hand slammed on the table. The chair smashed against the ground as she rose abruptly. Hot anger broiled her borrowed skin as she scolded herself for succumbing to sexual desire with a human form that was merely her *meal*. Her mind whirled as she focused, grasping for a way to get back her power and control. How could she have exposed herself like that?

She had to get control. She couldn't face another strike with Mordis.

She couldn't face another exorcism, either. Who would save her this time?

Addict

Blood oozed from the hole like red oil, spilling over soft flesh, pooling in the crease of Sage's arm. He stared in alarm. Hand shaking, he tried to pull the needle out of the well. He pulled. He pulled again. It wouldn't budge. Fresh blood burst at the disruption, running down his arm and over his fingers. Small pools of shiny scarlet formed in the series of hollows dotting his skin.

What the bloody hell?

No. It's not real.

He dropped his arms to his sides, leaned back against the wall, and stared across the room. The sounds of the other junkies lining the perimeter of the dark space whispered across his ears, a single desperate plea. Struggling to focus, he narrowed his eyes and found her. The old lady in the crooked and broken picture frame, her eyes jagged behind shattered glass.

He stared at the photo. He willed *her* to come. The evil being that had done this to him.

It was all clear now. It all made sense. It *was* her. The spikey, raven-haired, tatted-up rocker chick who had walked into his show, weeks ago, and turned his world upside down. She'd taken his energy. Somehow. It was *her* staring down at him from his stained ceiling, black ichor dripping from her eyes. She wasn't human. She was...supernatural...evil...*a demon.*

Sharp pain pierced his arm. He clenched his teeth and stared harder at the photo, glaring into the old woman's eyes, willing the demon with evil seeping from the black caverns where her eyes should be to appear.

The face behind the shattered glass morphed. The familiar hundred-year-old image appeared. The eyes spun, turning black. Spider legs oozed from the pupils, trickling over pallid cheeks. The mouth opened into a cavity, its depth daunting.

Sage tried to scream. *You.* His voice a mere whisper, he yelled again, but nothing came.

No. This isn't real. It isn't *fucking* real.

He took a deep breath, summoning every morsel of energy he still had. With all his might, he heaved himself to standing and stumbled across the room, his shaking hand extended in front of him, his blood-coated fingers reaching for her.

Finding his voice, he sputtered his words. "You. You did this. I'm coming for *you.*"

As he reached the photo, he traced his bloody fingertips across her face, smearing the dark gore with scarlet streaks. The face behind the glass shimmered, then vanished.

Sage grabbed the end of the syringe sticking wildly from his arm and yanked. It ripped free, tearing his flesh, spraying blood across the wall. He threw it to the ground. It smashed. Pieces flew.

A knocking sound echoed through the dim space. The cries of the desperate increased, closing in on him. The knocking grew louder.

He closed his eyes and pictured his apartment. The volume of the knocking increased. He concentrated, reaching for the sound.

FLESH EATER

A crisp *drip drip* echoed. A cold droplet landed on Elena's eyelid with a soft splash.

She opened her eyes.

A thick, shiny, red goo slathered the ceiling. Blood droplets hung, slowly pulling away, plunging to the cold, hard floor upon which she lay. One broke free, falling in slow motion toward her face. Frozen, she couldn't move her limbs. The viscous scarlet liquid landed on her face with a splat. It trickled down her cheek to the corner of her mouth. A metallic odour taunted her senses. Saliva pooled in the back of her throat.

Blinking hard, several times, she forced her heavy body to a sitting position and scanned her surroundings.

Fear clawed up her throat. An icy chill trickled down her neck, scraping frozen fingers over her back.

What the metal god fuck was going on?

Flesh. Flesh everywhere. Dripping with scarlet blood and translucent juices. Severed limbs, veins still pumping blue against pale flesh, tendrils of cartilage, bone, and tendon slithering through the thick air. Wet thuds as chunks of freshly torn flesh hit the floor sending soft copper sprays across her face. Scrapes of thin skin peeling away from fingers grasping for her. Tendrils of blood slithering down the rough contour of the concrete walls, pooling at the bottom in shiny disformed shapes.

A copper tinge clung to her nostrils and slithered across her tongue. She could feel crisp air, smell it, attempting to pierce the thick hot moist cloud engulfing the dim space.

Flesh. Blood. Everywhere. Around her.

Saliva drizzled down the corners of her mouth, pooling over the bottom of her chin, dripping onto her bare chest. She looked down at her body. She was naked. Red smears streaked her pale skin. Soil caked her hands and wedged underneath her fingernails.

A bloody chunk of fresh flesh pulsed beside her. Her stomach revolted; bile and unchewed meat lunged up her throat. She arched violently as hot vomit spewed from within, splashing over the flesh-and-blood-covered floor.

Panic grasped her demon soul. This wasn't what she was. It couldn't be. Her mind seized as she clawed at the memory of her demon life with desperate neurons.

A jolt. A cold rush.

Yellow rays of sunlight.

Sitting. At the table in her borrowed one-room apartment.

Elena bolted to standing; the chair crashed against the floor.

Her entire naked body, covered in a foul gloss of sweat, trembled.

She stumbled to the bedroom area, threw her silk housecoat around her, and sat hard on her bed.

A vision. It was only a vision. Why did Mordis have such control over her? He was punishing her. He was showing her what she was becoming. Or...what she had *been*. She screamed his name. All he gave her in return was silence.

A pounding against her chest, nails scraping her insides, down to the pit of her gut. Her hostess was restless. Elena was losing control.

Heat seethed through her pulsing veins as a fresh surge of anger and determination coursed through her. She was sick of this.

Elena stomped over to the table, sat down hard in a chair, and stared at a half-empty bottle of Fireball. Fluorescent rays streamed through the dirt-streaked window, casting a fragmented glow over the otherwise dark apartment. She released a long, pent-up sigh in a single, Fireball-tainted breath. She wrapped her cold fingers around the half-empty bottle, contemplating another pour. The potency of the cinnamon-infused liquor was subdued on her borrowed body, her demon essence coating the human blood veins with an ethereal armour. The effects were still there, faint, but present. Elena could feel a destructive desire pulsing within her evil soul, weaving thoughts of self-loathing through her borrowed brain, deep enough that she could feel them digging into her real mind, her demon mind.

The visions of her soil-caked hands and chunks of flesh dripping with blood had increased in vividness and frequency. At first, she thought Mordis was punishing her. Now she was convinced he was revealing her true nature. It explained everything.

Why he had found her digging into the soil of a grave in her nightgown when she was six years old. Why he'd been able to take her from the orphanage without a fight. Why she had cravings for flesh and blood.

The awakening of her true being must have occurred the night she drank the aura of Sage, the lead singer of Soiled Carcass. She knew something was off that night. She should have listened to her demon instincts. Nothing had been right since then. The insatiable hunger and thirst had weakened her. It had driven her to indulge on aura. To kill. To eat. To drink. She'd exposed herself. The weakness ravaging her demon body hung heavy over her heart.

Swiftly, she shook the thoughts away, yanked the cap off the bottle on the table, poured a double shot, and thrust the glass against her trembling lips caked in cherry remnants.

Her heart ached. Not the human heart that she had taken for a ride, but her demon heart, if she had one. She'd allowed herself the luxury all these years of living her shallow demon life. Relishing in the hunt of the ultimate metal god, rising above his followers, entrancing them with his raw yet angelic voice, hypnotizing them with his mere presence upon his neon-lit pedestal. Devouring the essence within him, perhaps to a point of slight danger to him, but never too far to leave a lasting impact. She'd traipsed along the tight wire, dipping as close to the end of the rope as possible, but never crossing it.

Until now.

Tingles still tickled her loins, remnants of the electrically charged jolts that fused life into her demon soul as she sucked the last drop of life-giving aura from Jake. The luscious, metallic taste of the first bite of him, carefully carved into a lean cutlet, lingered on the back of her tongue.

The ravaging hunger swelled in the pit of her belly now. A dryness only known to a barren desert cracked the linings of her throat. Reminders that her demoness demeanour was as borrowed as the body she wore at this very moment.

It was clear as the winter runoff on the side of a mountain. When Mordis found her, she was a ghoul child, digging the earth, seeking flesh. When she wandered off at night, it was her ghoul heart leading her, seeking to be what her destiny sought.

Her stomach roiled. She swallowed against the burning revolt as she grasped the sides of the table.

Were her true colours too vibrant for her to suppress? Would she succumb to the savage feasting of human flesh, her destined form contorting whichever beautiful-fleshed human she chose into the glowing-green grotesque being she had been, and perhaps was meant to be?

Her voice, stifled and weak, whispered through her mind. *No.*

A rage shot a ball of fire up her insides. Her voice clawed through the thick cloud holding it captive. She screamed, silently. *Nooo.*

She stood, the chair flying from the impact and crashing to the ground. She grabbed the bottle and thrust it across the room. It hit the wall. Crinkling echoed as glass shards rained through the room. One landed on Elena's foot, piercing her flesh. Red trickled over the pale skin. Her mouth watered. Saliva dribbled from the corner of her lips, seeping down her chin.

Mordis.

Why had he kept this from her all these years?

Had he ever planned to tell her?

Her massive detour from her demon ways had led him to reveal her true roots. There was no way in hell she'd let go.

She would have to feast on the most indulgent metal god aura. She'd have to drink until her demon being resurfaced, stifling out any remnant of a taste for flesh and blood like a boot grinding the last sparks of a dying fire.

It was the only way.

First, she would have to fight. Fight for control of her senses, her urges, her destiny.

Sage, the metal god, it had all started with him. She was sure of it. Something had awakened. She'd gotten off course. Lost her composure. No more. It was time for her to get a hold of herself.

As her mind buzzed with a new focus, doubt squeezed her demon heart. She knew what she needed to do. She could only hope, pray to the metal gods, that it wasn't too late to stomp out whatever had been awakened within her.

Intervention

A loud knocking jolted Sage. His eyes sprung open. Sweat trickled down his face.

His arms rested on the kitchen table. No needles. No bloody holes. The knocking heightened. It was coming from the door.

He stood and walked on shaky legs across the room. As he reached the door, he halted and took a deep breath, trying to compose himself. Had he really been in the dark room dripping with desperation? *No.* Impossible. Yet, it felt *real.* Junkie whispers echoed in his ears. Sharp pain throbbed through his veins. Cold sweat trickled down his back.

Loud pounding, more persistent.

He grabbed the doorknob, turned, and pulled.

Turbo, Steele, and Shark stood, staring at him, concern hijacking their faces. He couldn't help but smile.

"Guys." His arms dropped by his sides.

"Sage. We need to talk." Turbo led the charge. Sage had never seen him look more sincere.

"Yeah." Sage walked over to the table and slumped down into a chair.

His bandmates followed. They joined him around the table, shooting nervous glances at each other.

Steele tossed his long, dark hair behind his shoulders. "Listen...we, uh...oh hell with it, we're concerned about you. We..."

Sage raised a hand. "I know. I'm acting all fucked up."

Shark swallowed. "Ya are. If you're...listen, man, if you're using, we need to know."

"Is that what you think?" Sage sat back in his chair.

Turbo scanned the room. He shot a glance at Shark, then Steele. "Well, that's the thing. At first, we thought you were. After the show at Bad Idol, you acted weird. You pulled away. Stopped wanting to party with us. Only showed up when you had to. So, yeah, at first we thought you'd found the needle again. But it didn't add up." Turbo leaned his broad shoulders over the table, his black tank top tightening against his muscles.

"If you were using, you'd be right there in the party with us." Shark twisted a lock of glossy blond hair between his pointer and middle fingers.

"And there'd be signs. Shakes. Sweats. You know the drill." Steele's tongue toyed with the piercing in his lower lip.

"You were distant. Tired. But...you weren't acting like you were drugged up." Turbo leaned his arms on the table.

"I'm not." Sage wracked his brain for his next move. What the hell was he going to tell them? I've been invaded by some evil supernatural thing disguised as a rocker chick? I'm possessed by a fucking demon? They'd lock him in an asylum. "I can't explain. It's..."

"You have to." Turbo pleaded with his eyes. "You have *no* choice. We've decided. You either tell us what's going on or we're done."

Sage leaned back in the chair. It creaked under his muscular weight. He looked at them each in turn. They'd been with him for over five years, through his overdose, through his rock bottom...they were *Soiled Carcass,* for fuck's sake. They could take it.

Sage sighed and leaned over the table. "Fine. It did start at Bad Idol. Something really fucked up happened. When I fell to the stage, it was like the life had been sucked out of me. I saw the same thing happen to the lead singer of Carnal Assault, the week after. He fell to his knees."

"I saw that, when I came looking for you." Shark nodded.

"There was this woman, raven hair, spiked, and tattoos...she...she was there. Both times." Sage swallowed back the doubt clawing up his throat. Would they believe him?

"Dragon tattoos?" Shark asked.

"Yeah." Sage nodded.

"I saw her, when the Carnal Assault dude fell." Shark sat back in his chair and rested a red-booted foot on the opposite knee.

"Careening Corpse, Death Animal, Savage Seer, and Ten Steps to Hell. They all had similar experiences. Singer from Ten Steps to Hell saw the chick, right when it happened." Sage ran his hands through his tangled hair. "I sound fucking *crazy.* I swear, it's all true."

Steele sat back, his mouth twisted into a frown. "I dunno, man. I mean, how can a *chick* take away your energy? Like, without even touching you?"

"I know." Sage looked at each of them again.

Shark pursed his lips. "But it can't be a coincidence. You saw her. *Ten Steps to Hell* dude saw her. *I* saw her, man." He looked at Steele. "C'mon, let's hear Sage out."

Steele shook his head. "Fine, man, whatever."

Sage sat up and exhaled. "After the night I collapsed, it all started. Visions. Of this face. White, old, black eyes and mouth. Oily shit seeping from her eyes. I'd see it, on my ceiling, in the middle of the night."

Steele frowned. Shark's eyes widened. Turbo sat silent, expressionless.

"It got worse. I had these visions of being back in the junkie house. That day. When you guys found me. It was vivid. Like it was real. Like I was actually *reliving* it. Every moment. The needle sticking out of my arm. The room was exactly the same. Even the photo on the wall in the cracked frame." Sage clenched his jaw.

"Lifelike visions. I've heard of this shit, man. Some kind of *delusions.*" Shark flattened his hands on the table and stood. "Ya got somethin' to drink? This is some serious shit."

"Yeah. Fridge." Sage nodded to the refrigerator.

Shark walked across the room and opened the fridge door. He took out a bottle of Rolling Rock. "You got an opener?"

Sage smiled. "On the counter."

Shark looked at the counter, grabbed the *Kiss* trinket and laughed. "Oh right. Didn't you buy this, Turbo?"

Turbo squinted, then snorted. "Yeah."

Shark snapped the cap off and took a long swig. "You guys want one?"

Sage shook his head.

Turbo and Steele both nodded. Shark opened the door again and took out two more bottles. He snapped the caps off, then walked back to the table. He put the bottles down with a clink. Turbo and Steele grabbed them eagerly.

Shark sat with a thud. "Keep talking." He nodded at Sage as he chugged back more beer.

Sage slid the laptop over from the corner of the table and fired it up. It hummed loudly and emitted a wave of heat.

"Fuck, man. How old's that thing?" Turbo raised an eyebrow and took another swig of beer.

"Old. Still works. Look." Sage turned the laptop. A barrage of white faces smeared in black streaks bombarded the members of Soiled Carcass.

"Jesus." Turbo frowned.

"Fuck me." Shark took a long swig of beer.

"This is the face I see. On my ceiling. Searches all bring up the same thing. A demon." Sage looked at each of his bandmates in turn. Silence clung to the room. Sage stood, walked over to the kitchen, and grabbed the ichor-soaked tea towel. Returning to the table, he hung it in front of his bandmates. "This black stuff, it dripped on me when I saw her face." He shook his head and dropped the tea towel onto the table. "Fuck. I sound crazy."

Shark looked at him. "Tell us more."

Sage spun the laptop toward himself, typed madly, and brought up his research. Turning the laptop again, bile surged up his throat as he anticipated the response of the guys who meant more to him than anyone in the world. "I'm not the only one to experience this shit."

"Delusions." Shark leaned toward the screen. "Told you. I've heard of this shit. I had a cousin who went to some loony bin. They weren't sure what it was."

Steele narrowed his eyes.

Turbo sighed. "You don't seem mental, man."

"I don't know. Something's happening. This woman shows up. Then the exhaustion. And the noise. The odour." Sage ground his teeth.

"Odour?" Turbo asked.

"You guys smelled worse to me than ever at the show at Metal Panther. I left. Went to watch the opener. Carnal Assault." Sage ran his hands through his hair.

"Yeah," Shark said. "I had to come get you when Turbo went nuts."

Turbo glared, then took a swig of beer.

"Hey, it's cool, man," Shark continued. "Just puttin' this all together."

"We smell?" Steele asked.

"No. Not more than normal. It was like my senses were heightened. Everything smelled worse. Even though it didn't. And everything seemed louder." Sage shook his head. "Then the visions of me back in that junkie house started. I'm telling you...it's like I'm *there*. Like it's happening. Over and over. But then, I'm back here. No needles. Nothing." He pointed at the computer screen. "That's why I looked this shit up. Alternate realities." He sat back hard in the chair. It creaked.

Shark leaned in close to the screen. "Delusional disorder. *Shit.* It says here hallucinations and delusions are symptoms of schizophrenia. And demon possession. Fuck, man. Sounds like what happened to my cousin."

Steele frowned. "Seriously?"

"Dude. For real." Shark's eyes widened. "A couple of her doctors said that sometimes she spoke in a deep voice. Like something from hell."

"What?" Sage thought back to the night in his truck. The voice, soft, pleading for help. The other voice, deep, like something evil. "OK, hear me out. After I found out about the other bands, I figured out where she'd be. I went. Confronted her."

"What? Where?" Turbo leaned over the table.

"Velvet Owl. Triple header. Satan's Slut. Cranial Crave. Primal Pulse." Sage sighed.

Shark's eyes widened. "And?"

"She was there. I saw her go up to the stage, during the second band. Cranial Crave. It was all messed up. She did her *feeding* or whatever the fuck it is. I think she went too far. She collapsed. The crowd turned on her."

"Holy shit." Shark slapped the table. "So it's all over then?"

Sage shook his head. "No. I...I saved her."

"What the fuck, man," Turbo exclaimed.

"I know. I don't know what came over me. I felt *pulled.*" Sage wiped the sweat from his forehead with his hand.

"Then what?" Shark asked, excitement dancing in his eyes.

"I took her to my truck. Something really strange happened. Like she had some sort of hold on me. We fucked." Sage's stomach surged while tingles erupted in his loins.

"Fuck. Me." Shark smiled. "You fucked the evil thing that's invading you?"

"Yeah. Then...I confronted her. About me. And the others. She tried to leave. I grabbed her. Her skin, it burned. She seemed weak or something. This voice, a different voice than hers, it asked me for help. It said *she has me.*" Sage paused, running his hands through his tangled locks. He shook his head.

"Go on," Shark said.

Sage swallowed. "She turned on me. She hovered, in the air. Without touching me, she slammed me against the back of the cab. The glass cracked. She's got some sort of *powers*. Then her voice, it turned. Deep. Evil. Never heard anything like it."

Shark stood, grabbed his beer, and paced the room. "I *told* you. Some sort of evil spirit. You collapsed. The heightened senses. The visions. The *night terrors.* Levitation. A voice from hell. This *thing,* it's using that woman's body. You guys never heard about this before?"

"In movies, man, never thought this was real." Turbo lifted his bottle. It shook as he took a gulp.

Steele stood, slammed his beer on the table. "This is *insane.* You're bullshitting us."

"No. I'm not." Sage looked up at Steele, holding his gaze.

Shark walked back to the table and slammed his bottle down too. Beer spurted from the top. "Why the *fuck* would he make this up? Why would *I* make it up about my cousin?"

Steele leaned over the table, glaring at Shark. "Maybe he *is* all fucked up on drugs. Listen to this shit. Evil spirit?" He spun his fingers next to his ears like he was crazy. "Cuckoo. That's what you guys sound like."

"Look around you, man. Do you see any needles? Any sign of drugs? There's nothing." Shark strode across the room, waving his arms. "Look. Not a single fucking sign of drugs. If he was so fucked up, he wouldn't be able to hide it." He lifted the cushions on the couch, waving underneath. "Nothing."

Steele hesitated, his mouth twisting. He shook his head and grabbed his coat. "No. I'm outta here." He shot a glare at Sage. "You wanna get fucked up and pretend it's some kinda devil possessing you? Fine. I ain't got time for this shit."

Steele stormed out of the apartment. The door slammed behind him.

Shark looked at Turbo, then Sage. "So. How do we get rid of your demon lady?"

CALL THE DEVIL

E lena shot back the Fireball and swallowed hard. Sweat poured from her pores, over her face, and down her arms. Her palms pressed hard against the table. The glow of the moon trickled through the window, the only light in the otherwise dark apartment.

Chunks of bloody flesh still pulsed in her mind from the last vivid hallucination induced by Mordis. Wet splats still echoed through her thoughts. She couldn't take it anymore. She knew what she had to do.

The night she'd fed on Soiled Carcass, her ghoulish roots had been awakened within her. Tingles of lust burst through her loins as Sage's face glowed in her mind. The little girl ghoul within had clawed its way out. Her hunger for flesh and thirst for blood had surfaced. Ghoulish cravings for human touch had followed. All the rules that Mordis had imposed upon her had been a result of her *new* demon form, one she wasn't born with. Could it really be that he was only trying to protect her? The red glow of his eyes simmering in the back of her mind reminded her that if he did indeed have any *concern* for her at all, it had morphed into *power* and *control.*

It was time for *her* to take control.

She tilted her face toward the moon and uttered her call.

Asmodeus, Devil of Lust, I call upon you.

In my hour of need. I request your seed.

I beg for your mercy. I beg for your hand.

Guide me.

Take me.

I want to be yours.

The cracked crevices of her dry lips pressed together as she repeated her call, over and over, closing her eyes and feeling the celestial power of the moon's glow over her glistening face.

A crackle thundered through the room.

Elena's eyes bolted open. She sat silent.

Hot bursts of flame shot through the room. The flames dissipated. The outline of a face formed. A face like nothing Elena had ever seen.

Thin and pale with severe cheekbones protruding in sharp edges. Eyes narrowed, glowing hot and red, black pupils pulsing. Lips, pointed at the top, full and luscious at the bottom, glossed with scarlet. Horns weaving from the head in thick, contoured formations of hard bone, glowing red, etched in black.

The voice that followed echoed through the room like the calls from an ancient being reaching all ends of the earth.

"What is it you seek?"

Elena swallowed back the fear clawing at her throat. She licked her parched lips. Her voice, barely audible, cracked as she spoke. "Asmodeus. I seek to be your child."

The face thrust across the room, landing inches from Elena's. A cold washed over Elena's skin.

Drizzles of dark ichor slithered from the black pupils and down the ancient, pale face. The scarlet lips stretched into a sadistic smile. "*You.* Elena. Young demon. *You* seek to be *my* child?" A sinister laugh grabbed Elena's ears.

"Yes." Elena clenched her teeth. Her stomach roiled.

"*You.* A flesh eater. A *ghoul.* You seek to cast off your origins? You seek to become a full demon? A demon of lust?" The ichor streamed, thick and glossy, pooling in the cheekbones, drizzling over the scarlet lips.

Chunks of flesh invaded Elena's mind. The taste of blood on her lips taunted her. She gagged. *No.* She wasn't a ghoul. She was a demon. She knew with every demon ion buzzing through her borrowed human body, this was her real destiny.

"Yes." The conviction in her voice was real.

A black tongue slithered from Asmodeus' mouth and across her scarlet lips. "You have come a long way, you luscious little thing." Saliva pooled in the corners of her mouth. "You *might be* powerful enough." A black-nailed claw reached from thin air, running down Elena's face, sending cold, tantalizing tingles through her. "On your six-hundred-and-sixty-sixth day as a demon your origins were awakened. You must cast them off. You must commit entirely to *me.* You *must* make a *sacrifice.*" The face shimmered.

Heat swelled through the room. Sweat poured down Elena's face. The image of a girl, naked and trembling, flashed before her.

Demon Ritual

The celestial glow of the moon reached silver fingers through the entire one-room apartment. Tall, burgundy candles circled the perimeter of the room. Their orange-red flames hot and vibrant, wax dripped down their sides like the black demon blood slithering from Elena's eyes. She sat still and silent, staring at the human sacrifice in the centre of the room.

She grabbed the bottle of Fireball perched next to her and tilted it to a small glass. A cinnamon fire burned the back of her throat as potent liquid slid down her throat. She slammed the glass on the floor with a loud clank then tilted her head. Her borrowed eyes rolled into the rear of their sockets, exposing the black orbs of her demon eyes. Her face paled as it morphed into the six-hundred-and-sixty-six-year-old being hiding under its human skin mask. Bone protruded and claws pierced through the flesh of the hands caging her true form.

The voice of the death metal singer of Goatwhore, blasting from a boom box perched in the centre of the room, reached a climax in volume and intensity as the words of *Born of Satan's Flesh* echoed through the still space. The flames of the candles stretched higher, licking the cool air, wisps of heat hissing against the chill atmosphere clasping the room. Her sacrifice lay still. Elena had captured a young woman of the purest of humans, untouched by lust. Her virgin blood pooled beside her still, naked body.

It was time.

Time for Elena to take hold of her rightful form. The one she was promised as a little girl with shame in her eyes and fresh soil beneath her nails.

Her dark orbs, where eyes should be, glowed. Her cracked lips stretched open to reveal the cavern of darkness within. Her voice, a devilish growl, erupted through the room as she spoke.

I revoke all control from Mordiggian, The King of Ghouls, over my soul.

I beg for release from his cult of flesh eaters.

I call upon the power of Asmodeus, the Devil of Lust.

I ask to be embraced into the fold upon which I belong.

I commit to honour Asmodeus, from whose seed I have grown.

Allow me to feed upon your energy to transform into my true being.

A blast of cold chilled the room. Clouds of icy air wafted through the space.

The flames of the candles heightened. Bright bursts of orange reached for the ceiling.

The walls trembled. Dark, thick sludge dripped from the ceiling. Oily tendrils slithered down the walls.

The whole room breathed in response to Elena's chant, a long, deep breath of ice-cold evil.

Her satanic roots, called upon in her hour of need, strengthened her demon soul.

Her body shook. Her midnight lips trembled. Her dark pupils bled her demon life juice. As it trickled down her ancient, pallid face, her black tongue slithered across her cheek and licked the evil life juice.

Nearing the end of her ritual, her lips contorted into a grotesque smirk. Her demon voice, deep and raw, rumbled a laughter from the pits of hell. Her body rose, levitating several feet above the table, in the centre of the glowing flames.

Metal Demon Rise

The stench of cheap booze and piss clung to the air. It was hot and moist. Elena shot back her fifth Fireball and licked her top cherry lip as she winked at her after-dinner treat serving drinks behind the bar. Her chosen dive bar of the night, *The Glorious Beast,* was definitely glorious and it pulsed with a beastly energy.

Her demon blood broiled.

Her boots clanked across the beer-stained floor. Skin dripping with booze and sweat grazed her arms as she snaked her way through the crowd.

At the lip of the stage, she raised her hands, stretching her borrowed fingers toward the ceiling. Bones crackled and flesh tore as her demon fingers ripped through the human flesh holding them captive. A deep growl erupted from her throat as she scanned the pathetic metal maniacs banging their heads, beer sloshing from their cups as they raised their hands for the love of metal.

Elena no longer gave a flying metal fuck what she exposed. She was the fucking death metal demon, spawned from Asmodeus, and seeping with lust. She was the devourer of death metal aura.

A flash of psychedelic lightning tore across the room as she stretched her demon claws to their full length. The room darkened. Red dripped from the ceiling, slithering down the walls, pooling on the floor. The crowd cowered. Faces paled. Eyes widened.

The metal man leading the band on stage closed his eyes as he released a guttural screech. As she tilted her head back, Elena stretched the human lips caging her true form until they ripped. The black cavern of her demon mouth opened, seeking her power source. Blood-orange aura shot from the metal man's mouth as he froze in place, his body shuddering until it reached full convulsions. Black dripped from the aura, painting splash patterns of death on the floor.

Elena drank, long and hard, until her insides sizzled. Her mouth snapped shut with a wet slap.

The metal man crumpled to the ground. His bandmates stood stunned. Parts of the crowd huddled together, cowering in the corners of the walls. Those who broke free ran for the door, causing a bottleneck of hot, sweaty bodies sliding against each other in desperation.

Elena raised her six-hundred-and-sixty-six-year-old face to the ceiling as she exhaled. A sinister laugh vibrated up her throat and out her open mouth. She looked around the room. Her neurons buzzed as panic and raw fear infused the air around her. *This.* This is what she was capable of, when Mordis wasn't holding her back. She could stay. She didn't need to. She'd drank enough to put her tank on full for a while.

It was good to feel like herself again.

Licking the remnants of her feast from the corners of her cherry-caked lips, she walked up to the bar. The bartender stood, jaw clenched, clutching a white towel in one hand, a beer glass in the other.

"How about one for the road?" Elena smiled and leaned over the bar as her supernatural being retreated back into the human form.

The bartender nodded. He grabbed a glass, filled it with cinnamon fire, and slid it across the bar.

The spicey burn soothed her throat. She winked at the bartender, spun on her heel, and made her way to the door.

Metal Men Unite

Empty bottles of Rolling Rock cluttered the kitchen table. Burger wrappers and fry boxes crumpled in the crevices of the cracked pleather couch. The room smelled of body odour, cheap beer, and grease.

Sage walked over to the window and flung it open. "You guys stink."

"Tell us something we *don't* know." Shark sneered.

"I thought your senses were amplified." Turbo leaned over the table, scanning all the clippings, notes, and print-outs they'd gathered.

Shark shook his head, his hair, still glossy despite the hours they'd been holed up in the apartment, brushing his shoulders. "Exhaustion. Heightened senses. Sound. Smell. Visions. Night terrors. Your greatest fears revealed." He took a swig of beer. "It all adds up."

Sage joined them at the table. "You guys don't think I'm a lunatic?"

Turbo shook his head. "At first, yeah. I thought maybe Steele was right. You'd gotten real good at hiding your habit." He took a pull from the bottle in his hand. "But...you ain't showing no signs of returning to your junkie persona."

Shark nodded. "Not even a stray needle *anywhere*. And you're too *together*, man."

"Shark saw her too. And that other singer..." Turbo set his bottle on the table with a loud clank. "And...what she did to you, in your truck. Some sort of power, without even touching you, man."

"I could be making this all up." Sage ran his hands through his hair as he paced back and forth. "Or imagining it."

"Nah. You're far too lucid." Shark looked Sage in the eyes. "We've got five metal men falling to their knees mid-performance. Six, including you, one week apart. That's a huge fucking coincidence."

"We've *got* to find out if this shit is real." Turbo walked to the window and took a deep breath of fresh air. "We *do* stink."

Sage laughed. "So, now what?"

Shark spoke. "That other voice, the one asking for help. There's someone in there, man. I told you, this *thing,* it's using this woman's body. As a host. It all sounds so much like what happened to my cousin, man." He slid a couple of pages across the table and examined them. "It's all right here. *Exorcism."*

"Fuck. This is crazy," Sage said. "But...that face. Like some ancient being. The eyes. The black shit dripping from them."

"It's demon blood. That's what it says here." Shark pointed at a page, intensity in his blue eyes.

Turbo spun and faced them, his tank top pulling against his broad shoulders. "Man, if this *thing* is real, if it has that woman...she needs help. And...how else are we gonna stop what's happening to *you*. To the other singers." He looked at Shark. "What happened to your cousin?"

Shark sat back in his chair. "They didn't know what to do. Died in the institute."

Turbo slammed his palms on the table. "Exorcism it is."

"If she's still sticking to this schedule...we can find her. But..." Sage paused.

"No, man. We gotta *lure* her in. We have to be in control. It's all here." Shark spun a page around and pointed at printed words.

Sage picked the page up and read it. "We need...the *name* of the demon..." He paused. "Elena."

"Elena?" Turbo asked.

"Doesn't sound like a demon name," Shark said.

"Yeah, I know. I went back to Bad Idol, talked to this bartender who went home with her, the night I first saw her. Said her name was Elena." Sage clenched his teeth.

"What? So we know where she lives," Turbo exclaimed.

"No. He couldn't remember. Said he was drunk." Sage frowned.

"Dammit." Turbo grabbed his bottle of Rolling Rock.

"The names of the devils..." Sage shuffled through the papers on the table. "Here. Lucifer, pride. Mammon, greed. Asmodeus, lust." He looked up from the words.

"She's spilling sex..." Turbo smirked.

"Is her name really Asmodeus?" Shark asked.

"I dunno," Sage said.

"OK. Elena. Asmodeus..." Shark grabbed the list again. "Whoever the fuck she is, how do we *lure* it in?"

"We put on a show," Turbo exclaimed.

"Show?" Shark asked.

"Yeah. She goes to the metal shows. Feeds on the front men. We offer up a show that she can't resist." Turbo smiled.

"So, you haven't fried all your brain cells." Shark chuckled.

"Brilliant." Sage nodded.

"We need this shit." Shark slid a printed page into the middle of the table.

Turbo leaned over and inspected it. "Holy water. Cross, made of metal. Bible excerpts. *What the fuck...*"

"I dunno. This is, like, out of some horror flick. You think this will really work?" Sage ran his hands through his hair. Oil coated his fingers. When was the last time he'd showered?

"No." Shark sat back in his chair and crossed his arms. "She's a *mutation*. Demons possess. Take over a body. The spawn of the devil himself. This religious shit forces the demon out. This one...she's got her own poison."

Sage narrowed his eyes. "Death metal singer." He sat down in the chair next to Shark.

"Exactly." Shark slapped his palms on the table. He leaned toward Sage. "You gotta remember the details of what happened in your truck. You said you were *pulled*. You said she seemed out of sorts after your wild ride."

"Yeah. She did. Like...she was just as shocked as I was," Sage said.

"Details. Think. Hard." Shark loomed closer.

Sage leaned back in his chair and closed his eyes. He shuffled through the images from the night in his truck with the demon. If that's what the fuck she was. The pull had been overwhelming. It was as if someone else was in his body, making the moves. Had she possessed him then and there? The lustful ride was like nothing he'd ever experienced. Like he was in another world. When it ended, she looked confused. Shocked. She tried to leave. He grabbed her. Her skin. It sizzled. Like it was burning.

His eyes shot open. "Her skin. Remember, I told you, it burned."

"What?" Turbo's eyes grew wide.

"Yeah. I swear, I had no control over my body. After she *seduced* me...or whatever the fuck she did...I came to. She *did* look confused. She tried to slip out of the truck. I grabbed her arm. I was coated in sweat. A lot of sweat. My arm grazed her skin. It sizzled." Sage paused.

"Your sweat." Shark shuffled through the printouts. "Here. The holy water is what is most pure to the typical demon. *Pure.* Maybe the death metal man sweat is what is *pure* to your little demon."

"Really?" Sage asked. Doubt swelled in his mind.

Turbo took a huge swig of beer then slammed the bottle on the table. "Whatever, man. I say we go with it. *Anything* that seems possible, let's just fucking do it."

Shark nodded. "Yeah. Let's go through this list of exorcism shit again. Use our brains, man. Figure out what might work on this demon."

Sage smiled. "You guys...what if this *is* all in my mind? Like, I *am* fucking crazy?"

Shark put the print-outs down and leaned back over the table. "Then we'll come visit you in the mad house, when this is all over."

"Yeah," Turbo said. "But first we need to find out. Are you crazy? Or are you possessed?"

Sage's shoulders relaxed. Soiled Carcass, minus a drummer, was in.

A pounding at the door jolted them all.

Sage thrust from his chair and bolted across the room. He yanked the door open.

Steele, his long, dark hair in a bulbous bun at the top of his head, sweat pouring down his face, stood with a stunned look. "I saw her."

"Who?" Sage motioned for Steele to come into the apartment.

Steele shuffled through the doorway. "Your demon. At *The Glorious Beast*."

Sage took a long, deep breath. Soiled Carcass was now *all in*.

Dripping Eyes and Exorcist Tools

Black ichor dripped from the eyes on the ceiling, stretching toward Sage like black tentacles.

He threw off the covers and bolted from the bed. He couldn't take it anymore. He strode to the kitchen, yanked open the fridge, and grabbed a bottle of Rolling Rock. He paused to look at the white-faced, black-eyed cat-man bottle opener, smiling at the thought of Turbo and the rest of his bandmates.

After chugging half the beer, he walked over to the table and inspected the lineup of items they had gathered for the impending death-metal exorcism. Vials of clear liquid, which they hoped was pure enough to sizzle the skin of the rocker-chick demon. Print-outs of chants that were supposed to force a demon from a human body. Pages with their own crudely written words, their attempt as death metal song writers to produce the lyrics that would exorcise a demon with exquisite taste.

Sage plunked down in a chair. The wood creaked under his muscular weight. He leaned back and took a long swig, trying to calm his nerves.

Once Steele had chugged a beer and calmed down a notch, he'd told them about his evening at The Glorious Beast. He'd witnessed their metal demon feasting on the death metal front man of Rancid Cross. He said black blood dripped from the walls as people piled through the exit, screaming and pushing. The demon lady was the spitting image of the photos that Sage had shown them. Steele had ran all the way here, not even able to think about what he was doing.

They'd called up the lead singers of Carnal Assault, Ten Steps to Hell, Careening Corpse, Death Animal, and Savage Seer. They had all been submersed in the same white-faced, black-eyed hallucinations dripping dark blood from their ceilings as Sage had. They'd all been living their own delusional hell, reliving the worst part of their lives. Over and over. They'd all heard about what happened at The Glorious Beast. They were eager to join the show that Sage and the rest of Soiled Carcass was planning.

In addition to this strong lineup of death metal men, the lead singers of Pestilential Flesh and Cranial Crave had been added to the roster. Apparently, they'd had similar experiences at shows over the last few weeks.

Sage picked up a vial of his own juices and held it in his palm.

If he was crazy, then so were all these other metal singers. Doubt clawed at his internals. Cold sweat trickled down his back. There was no turning back now. He prayed to the metal gods that he was strong enough to lead his fellow metal men into the most fucked-up performance of his life.

Killer Show

Elena took a long drag of the chill night air. Sage's face shimmered through her thoughts. The fucking leader of Soiled Carcass. The metal god who could hypnotize an entire room with his screeching wails. The sight of his luscious golden locks and bare torso rippling with muscles, his emerald eyes boring into her evil soul, his voice, something from the heavens yet edged with a razor-sharp rawness, all of it had heightened ghoulish longings that her birthday had brought to the surface.

The chains dangling over the pleather caging her curvaceous hips jangled as she stomped across the pavement. Deep bass rumbled up ahead. A red neon sign pulsed over a black door. *Velvet Plume.* She'd never been here before. Only read about it. For months, the abandoned warehouse had undergone major reconstruction to turn it into the hottest new live-music venue for those who liked it rough and loud. She'd been following the updates during her meticulous meal planning, but it had slipped off of her radar in her hunger and thirst infused haze as her inner ghoul had tried to claw its way to the surface.

Elena's heart pumped hard against her human chest. Her hostess had been restless ever since the hunger pains had started. The rocker chick – *fucking Pam* – had almost surfaced, breaking through Elena's devilish hold, a couple of times. The flames in hell would have to be frosted with ice before Elena would let the weakling get in her way. She took a deep breath, closed her eyes, and raised her hands. The stars overhead flickered. The moon dimmed, then brightened. Elena's hostess quieted as Elena slammed her back in her box. There would be no interruptions tonight.

Shaking off the tiny glitch in her schedule, Elena stomped toward the black door. The bass rumbled louder as electric guitar wailed and a savage beat hijacked her heart.

She yanked the door open and thrust her human body into the space.

The door slammed shut behind her. Darkness grabbed her.

What the holy fuck?

A single spot was illuminated ahead, up on a stage. A light flickered, glowing over a face. Long, golden locks flittered in a breeze. *The voice.* It had invaded her demon soul the first time she'd heard it. It had an even more severe effect on her now. Her body shuddered as the raw-edged voice slithered tantric tendrils into her borrowed body, stretching, grasping for her demon soul.

Cold prickles crawled up her back. Sage continued to serenade her, his voice building toward a climax, reaching a screech from the pits of hell. He devoured her with his eyes, boots rooted to the stage, muscles rippling down his bare chest.

She narrowed her eyes and licked her cherry lips. Her demon blood seared her human veins. He would not win. She prowled into the darkness, toward the stage, eyeing the edges of the room. No movement. Were they alone? What was he doing here?

She smirked. Gore Casket wasn't playing tonight. Neither was Evil Candle or Hate Pit. Sage had lured her here. She should have smelled it the moment her eyes landed on the neon flyer.

A light clicked on, illuminating a brown-haired, broad-shouldered drummer, perched high on a black-and-silver drum set. He pounded out a savage beat. Another light followed, revealing a long, dark-haired, sinewy man strumming a rumbling line across the thick strings of a black bass tipped in orange flames. A third light glowed over a blond-haired man in red boots, his fingers flying across the strings of a metallic-blue guitar. *Soiled Carcass* in their full glory.

As she reached the centre of the room, a series of flickering lights broke through the darkness around her. She was in the middle of a circle comprised of metal men. Some of them looked faintly familiar.

Before she could form a thought, the assault began.

Their arms rose. Their hands plunged forward, shooting streams of clear liquid at her. Droplets landed on her face and her arms. Her skin sizzled. Threads of smoke swirled from her burning flesh. *What the holy hell?* The scent of man mixed with death metal tantalized her nostrils as the droplets of human fluids evaporated from her crackling skin.

She twisted her black lips into a contorted smirk and laughed a deep, guttural sound. "The pure life liquid of the death metal gods. Those upon whom I *feast*."

They launched a second assault without hesitation. Arms flung. Long hair whipped. Clear liquid, extracted from their own bodies, landed with loud, hissing splashes on the epidermis that Elena's demon soul was caged within. Sizzling and crackles stung the air. Her guttural laugh faded into a moan. Whisps of smoke rose off the pleather caging her legs as the purity of the metal man sweat disintegrated the material, finding the flesh beneath.

Searing pain sliced through Elena's borrowed body, reaching for the demon within. Her hostess became restless, turning aggressive as she tossed and turned and clawed at the cage Elena had put her in. Fucking Pam, aware of her situation, was fighting for the body she rightfully owned.

Elena shuddered as the pain pricked her demon soul. There was no way in the burning depths of hell she was going to let this happen. Hot, hellish anger broiled within, disintegrating the bites of pain caused by these metal men turned exorcists. They should have stayed on stage, clinging to the idea of being some sort of god clutching a microphone.

Elena's anger boiled over. Hot evil surged through her demon veins, turning her human veins deep purple. She closed her eyes, took a deep breath, and slammed her hostess back in her cage. Her borrowed body shuddered, then stilled.

When she opened her eyes, the circle of metal men had closed in on her. Sage jumped down from the stage.

In a death metal screech, the words slipped from his mouth. "Elena. *Asmodeus.* In the name of *Possessed, Death, Necrophagia, Obituary, Autopsy, and Morbid Angel,* I command you to release your hold on death metal men. I command you to depart from this human form."

The names of the death metal pioneers stung her ears. Her name, spoken in his powerful voice, ripped at her heart. *How the metal fuck did he know her name?*

She slammed her palms over her burning ears.

The sounds of Soiled Carcass increased in volume, building a rumbling bass line, a high-voltage guitar riff, and a savage beat.

Sage repeated his death wail. The metal men surrounding her joined. Death metal voices merged into one. Half song, half screech, raw edged and pure. They formed a circle around her. A front of metal men. The tone of the voices turned. No longer speaking, their voices blended into a single death metal melody, building as their eyes bored into her.

They caged her in the centre of their circle, looming toward her, raising their hands, dousing her in another pour of pure human liquid. Sizzling strips of skin peeled away from Elena's face and arms. She tried to laugh, but her demon voice caught in the back of her throat. She could feel scraping inside her borrowed body as her hostess clawed her way out of her box. Pam's voice surfaced in a desperate wail. "Heeelp meee..."

The metal men halted.

"We're hurting her." The one with a wild orange-red mane stilled.

Sage glared at him. "Keep going. We can't stop until the demon releases the human."

His voice rose as he repeated the chant. The voices of the metal gods merged into pure power, aimed at the evil being in the centre of the circle.

"Elena. *Asmodeus.* In the name of *Carnage, God Macabre, Entombed, Dismember, Grave, and Unleashed, we* command you to depart from this human form."

Elena's demon being shuddered. She launched her own assault and surged a wave of broiling heat through her borrowed body. Her hostess screamed.

The metal man with raven hair and dark eyes stepped into the circle. "We have to help her."

Sage yelled, "Don't get any closer."

The metal man stepped back in line.

Sage reignited the chant. The wails of the metal gods drowned Elena's. They closed the circle in on her tighter. Her thoughts blurred. She cowered into a corner of her borrowed body and eased up on her hold.

Her hostess cried; tears streaked down her cheeks. "I'm in here. P-p-please...make her stop."

The metal screech heightened, turning raw and guttural. The circle tightened.

"Elena. *Asmodeus.* In the name of *Mogis,* death metal god, *we* command you to depart from this human form."

Elena slipped further and further into the recesses of her borrowed body, releasing her evil grip over her hostess. She closed her eyes and drank in the vibrations of *the voice.* Sage. Lead singer of Soiled Carcass. The metal god who had changed her world, heightening the ghoulish desires that had been simmering within her. Primal urges to eat flesh and drink blood. Lustful cravings she'd never experienced. Her demon being shuddered with tantric tingles. She looked up at the circle of death metal elite, closing in on her fast.

A fresh wave of energy shot from Elena's demon soul. Her borrowed body levitated over six feet into the air, hovering over the metal men.

They looked up at her with panic in their eyes. Their chanting heightened, roaring into a death metal wail.

The rocker chick, Elena's hostess—*fucking Pam*—fell to the ground. Her head hit the floor with a wet thud. Her body went limp.

Heavy Metal Exorcism

Voices flittered through the dark room, as if in a dream, or deep into the far end of a long tunnel.

"Is she OK?" A blurry image of long, raven hair.

"She's not breathing." The fuzzy outline of an orange-red mane.

"No pulse." *The voice.* It was the voice that had started all of this.

"Damnit, I think we lost her." Glossy, blond locks flittered.

"Is the demon gone?" Charcoal wisps of hair flew.

Silence. Faces glimmered under the lights. Long hair hung in luscious waves.

They stood, in turn, forming a small circle around the lifeless body.

Sage wheezed between heavy breaths.

"You OK, man?" long, black hair asked.

They raised their lights toward Sage's face. As he exhaled, his eyes rolled back in his head, revealing dark orbs. His flesh crinkled in upon itself, a sickly grey hue tinged his face. His mouth opened, stretching his lips unnaturally wide, forming a dark, unending cavern.

"What the fuck, man," Raven Hair asked.

"It has him." Orange-red mane's voice quivered.

The metal men jerked back in a swarm of erratic movements.

Sage unleashed a steady blood-orange glimmering stream speckled with black. It surrounded the makeshift exorcists. His head flung back, his long, blond locks whipping through the air. His muscled arms went limp. The vial of death metal liquid slipped from his grip, hitting the ground and shattering into a million pieces, droplets spraying. His legs lifted; his torso fell back. His body, now vertical with the ground, levitated several feet upward, then hovered. The remaining metal men halted in their tracks, mouths dropping, as they looked up at their leader.

As she entered Sage, something within her demon soul lit up with electricity. Her neurons sizzled. Her brain buzzed. Her heart pumped faster than a hummingbird's.

You bitch. Sage thrust his thoughts at her.

You weak junkie. Elena laughed.

She summoned a ring of blazing fire and circled the flames around his voice. He tried to grab his throat. She constrained his arms to his sides. With a forceful blow, she slammed the blazing fireball into a box. His death metal wail and mortal soul followed.

With a full grip on her new host, Elena spoke with a low, thunderous growl, "You think you can outwit me? *Cocksuckers.*"

Sage's lips turned black then stretched into a grotesque grin. A hellish laugh rumbled from within.

"Holy shit." The raven-haired metal man's face went pale.

"Now what?" Blondie flung his metallic-blue guitar over his back, his lips quivering.

The man with orange-red hair raised his vial and continued with his chant. One by one, the others followed.

Elena erupted with more grinding laughter. Sage's head spun as she shot her black-orb gaze around the circle. An ice-cold blast escaped her lips, seeping through the air in a thin, white mist.

Ice crystals formed on their faces. One by one, they fell to their knees. Vials hit the ground, shattering into minuscule pieces, particles of sweat turning to dust.

The metal men clutched their throats. Black sludge projected from their mouths, shooting to the centre of the circle, splashing into a colossal pool. A black mist sprayed through the air. Viscous liquid dripped from their faces and their long hair.

Leave them alone. Sage's voice slammed against Elena's ears. She jolted at the unexpected intrusion. She pushed harder, forcing him into his cage. Her body trembled with the exertion. Why was he so strong?

Moans erupted from the men, on their knees, in a circle, coated in black sludge.

Elena raised her borrowed hands. Iridescent lightning flashed through the dark room. The walls rumbled. She shot an evil glare at each of the men in turn.

Their mouths morphed, contorting into grotesque shapes. Their moans heightened into panicked screams. The flesh of their mouths softened, like wax dripping down a candle. Their malleable skin mutated, sewing their mouths shut, muffling their screams.

One by one, the metal gods were silenced forever. Panic seeped from their eyes. Their hands clutched their throats and clawed at their faces. Ichor-stained tears trickled down their faces.

Metal gods, my ass.

Stop it! Sage's scream shattered Elena's thought. How the *fuck* was he breaking through the demon hold she had on him?

Fuck off, junkie. You're only as good as your last needle. Scum. She slammed him back in his box, again. Sweat trickled down her borrowed face—Sage's face—soaking his hair and dripping from his chin.

The moans of the metal men heightened. They clawed at their melted mouths, their shoulders trembling.

This is between you and me, demon bitch, Sage screamed in a death metal wail. Elena fell to her knees. *What the metal fuck?*

Enough. Junkie. She tilted Sage's head, rolling his eyes into the back of his head. Red glowed from the edges of her black demon eyes, now fully exposed in his human sockets. Her demon fingers stretched, ripping the skin of his human appendages. Her claws, now fully exposed, reached up to the ceiling. Fluorescent lightning struck again, illuminating the entire room in a blue flash. Her body rose into the air, hovering over the metal men all on their knees, still clawing at their sewn-shut mouths in complete desperation.

She could still hear Sage, wailing a faint death metal screech. She closed her eyes and took a deep breath, causing the walls to shudder. Black-red streams trickled down them. With all her demon force, she took a final swing and slammed Sage hard against the insides of his own body. He went silent.

Her eyelids fluttered, then opened. A glowing-red rim pulsed around her glassy, midnight eyes. She inspected the circle of men, once metal gods on a neon stage, now on their knees, unable to utter a single lyric.

Her laugh erupted from the pit of her belly, deep and rolling, up her throat, out her mouth, vibrating through the cold air and shaking the walls.

The death metal wails of the metal men were now mere whispers. Their nails ripped gashes in their faces as they continued to claw at their morphed and melted mouths. Elena smirked as she stared at them. The flesh of their fingers dripped away from their hands. Their muted moans subsided. Terror seeped from their faces.

Their skin drizzled down their arms. Their limbs melted into their torsos. Their torsos into their legs. Flesh fell in chunks, landing with loud splats in the thick pool of black ichor. The metal men disintegrated into a basin of melted flesh and blood.

Elena took a deep breath in, then exhaled an ice-cold stream of white air.

Her host was silent.

Fresh Meal

H e was a well-behaved host.

Not even the slightest whisper of a death metal wail had slithered through the inside of his body. Elena was pleased.

It was time to tap into his voice once again. *The voice* that had started the whole series of events that had led her here.

She moved her borrowed body, tall, muscular, and powerful, across the stage. Sweat trickled down the ripples of her bare chest, seething with masculinity. Long, luscious locks of golden hair hung over her broad shoulders. A guitar rumbled behind her. A savage drumbeat followed. She shot a glance at each of the members of *Metal Flesh,* the hottest new band blasting the roof off all the local joints. After all, when the lead singer of an uprising band loses all his bandmates to an unfortunate night of drug overdoses and an accidental fire in an abandoned warehouse, he must move on.

Taking her newfound place centre stage, she raised her arm and brought the microphone to her lips. Tapping into the vocal abilities of her host, Sage, the once lead singer of Soiled Carcass, she brought his voice to life again.

The crowd went wild.

Their savage energy sent electric shocks through her borrowed body, all the way to her demon soul. She'd never felt more alive.

As the first track of the night neared its end, she took a moment to breathe in the essence of the room. Her eyes scanned the crowd, perusing the plethora of potential meals. Now that she was a full demon, there were *no rules*. She could feed on, drink from, and fuck anyone she wanted. As her gaze drifted to the edge of the closely cluttered pack, her demon being jolted.

Mordis. At the very back, lingering by the bar, sipping casually from a glass of rich, caramel liquid. She smirked. He raised his glass and winked at her.

She didn't think she'd ever see him again, since she'd summoned all her power and will and asked for release from his hold. He was Mordiggian, the King of Ghouls. He'd saved her. He could have forced her to be the ghoul she should have been. Instead, he'd shown her an alternate path for her evil soul, one that she craved. Now, here he stood, giving her his final blessing to fully embrace her death metal demon destiny.

Raising the microphone, she summoned the power of her host and belted out a death metal screech.

Acknowledgments

Writing a book is not a solo effort. If you helped me out in any way at all with a warm hug, a cold beer, a word of encouragement, a head bang, a sweaty night of dancing, or some honest feedback, thank you from the bottom of my heart.

A special thank you to Taija Morgan for inspiring me with her own delightful demon books, for her always amazing and meticulous feedback, and for her ever so entertaining reactions and comments.

A massive thank you to Cami Schulte and Anita Luszszak for reading outside of their realms, demolishing early copies of this book, and providing honest and helpful feedback.

A head bang (or two) in honor of *Osyron* and *Dark Divine* for the inspiration from your killer videos and your double killer live performances.

A loving thank you to James Hiner for showing me how to stretch my limits, to try things even when I am hesitant, and for tolerating the death metal blasting through the house.

About Author

Julie Hiner spent endless hours during her childhood lost in the pages of books. The only thing that took precedence over a book was her Walkman. Julie remains a hardcore 80s rocker at heart.

Julie worked as a computer scientist, specializing in network simulation. On a break between contracts, she published an inspirational work of nonfiction, her own story of facing fear and anxiety on a bicycle in the European mountains.

Julie now writes psychological horror/suspense heavily infused with hard rock and metal. She has published an *80s metal murder* detective series, a 90s nostalgic serial killer novella, co-curated a horror anthology, and had several horror short stories published in anthologies. You can find her at KillersAndDemons.com serving up toxic cocktails of metal and murder.

Also By

Detective Mahoney Series:
Final Track – Book 1
Acid Track – Book 2
Back Track – Book 3
Devil's Track – Book 4
Dead End Track – M.E. Blackwood Story
Novellas:
Owen's Terrarium – Killers and Demons
Anthologies:
The Omens Call – Edited by Hiner and Willcocks
Short Stories:
Ice Metal Queen, Solstice in Purgatory, The Seventh Terrace
Attic Puppet, Terrors From The Toy Box, Phobica Books
Candy Lady, October Blood, Hawke Haus Books
Hallowed Killer, Pulp Harvest, Blood Rites Horror
Corpse Forest, The Other Side, Devil's Rock Publishing
Tuny, Terrace VI: Forbidden Fruit, The Seventh Terrace

THANK You

Thank you for reading this book.

If you enjoyed *Metal Demon* please consider leaving a review Goodreads, Bookbub, or your retailer of choice. A review is worth a lot to an author.

Come visit @ KillersAndDemons.com